ABOUT THE AUTHOR

When Geoffrey McSkimming was a boy he
found an old motion-picture projector and a tin
containing a dusty film in his grandmother's attic.
He screened the film and was transfixed by
the flickering image of a man in a jaunty pith helmet,
baggy Sahara shorts and special desert sun-spectacles.
The man had an imposing macaw and a clever looking
camel, and Geoffrey McSkimming was mesmerised
by their activities in black-and-white Egypt, Peru,
Greece, Mexico, Sumatra, Turkey, Italy and
other exotic locations.

Years later he discovered the identities of the trio,
and he has spent much of his time since then retracing
their footsteps, interviewing surviving members of the
Old Relics Society, and gradually reconstructing these
lost true tales which have become the enormously
successful Cairo Jim Chronicles.

While retracing Cairo Jim's footsteps for *Cairo Jim
and the Chaos from Crete*, Geoffrey McSkimming also
discovered some startling facts about what went on,
thousands of years ago, at King Minos' palace in
Crete. This information was known by Jim of Cairo,
but was never published or spoken of outside the walls
of th

For Belinda,
who walked with me above the
Cretan Labyrinth...

First published in Great Britain 2008 by Walker Books Ltd
87 Vauxhall Walk, London SE11 5HJ

2 4 6 8 10 9 7 5 3 1

Text © 2002 Geoffrey McSkimming
Cover illustration © 2008 Martin Chatterton

The right of Geoffrey McSkimming to be identified as author of
this work has been asserted by him in accordance with the
Copyright, Designs and Patents Act 1988.

This book has been typeset in Plantin

Printed in Great Britain by
Clays Ltd, St Ives plc

British Library Cataloguing in Publication Data:
a catalogue record for this book is available from the British Library.

ISBN 978-1-4063-1046-7

www.walkerbooks.co.uk

CAIRO JIM

AND THE CHAOS FROM CRETE

A Tale of Underground Uncertainty

GEOFFREY McSKIMMING

WALKER
BOOKS

▲▲▲▲▲ CONTENTS ▲▲▲▲▲

Part One: FOR SO LONG OUT OF MIND

1 CUTTING IT FINE! 9

2 YOU NEVER KNOW... 22

3 MILLICENT SPULE IS ALARMED! 31

4 RENEGADES IN THE RUBBLE 47

5 LORE OF THE LABYRINTH 59

6 INTO THE MAZE 71

7 A TALOS TO ABUSE 84

Part Two: GREATER THAN ZEUS HIMSELF

8 KNOSSOS IN A FUG 93

9 THE DESIGN OF DAEDALUS 107

10 HOURS OF TORCHLIGHT 115

11 TURNING A CORNER IN TIME 127

12 AXE ME THAT AGAIN 135

13 A TWINGE IN JAIPUR 147

14 SHADOW IN THE DARKNESS 151

15 GLOOM WITH A VIEW 157

16 ALMIGHTY CLANGER 169

17 HOW THE MIGHTY HAVE FALLEN 180

18 MISUNDERSTOOD 188

19 THE EMBERS OF DAWN 200

Knossos

Take all our horrible monsters
and fling them far from here,
where frail and fickle memory
might make them disappear –
but heed the march of History
and bear its strength in mind:
those monsters, rank, abominable
a different light may find…

(Thought to have been written by Cairo Jim, and found by Geoffrey McSkimming tucked away inside a crumbling book in the library of the Old Relics Society, Cairo, Egypt.)

Part One:

FOR SO LONG
OUT OF MIND

◇ ◇ ◇ ◇ ◇ **1** ◇ ◇ ◇ ◇ ◇

CUTTING IT FINE!

"THE LOST TOMB OF SNIP-HOTEP, Royal Hairdresser to Queen Nefertari. I can't believe we've found it!"

Cairo Jim, the well-known archaeologist and little-known poet, held his kerosene lantern above his pith helmet and stared at the beautiful tomb before him. Five seconds ago he had become the first person to enter this place in the Valley of the Hairdressers, Upper Egypt, in over three thousand years.

"Raaaark!" squawked Doris the macaw, perched on his shoulder. Her small eyes were as wide as they could be, and she was jerking up and down excitedly.

"What do you think, my dear?" Jim asked her as he moved the lantern's glow across the hieroglyph-covered walls.

Doris blinked and put her head to one side. "It's a lot more ornate than I'd imagined," she answered. "I had no idea that a mere hairdresser would've got such grand wall decorations."

"Ah, but he wasn't any *ordinary* hairdresser. Oh no. He was the personal stylist to the Queen. People believed that he held special place in her court. She used to tell him state secrets and royal gossip and all

sorts of things that no one else – not even the High Priests – were told."

"He was her favourite?"

"So it seems." Jim raised the lantern beam higher, and studied the beautiful ceiling. It was deep blue and decorated with thousands of painted stars and tiny pairs of golden scissors.

"And then he died," Doris said.

"Er… you *could* put it like that."

Doris looked at him. "You mean … he *didn't* die?" She gulped, and her yellow-and-blue feathers began to hackle.

"Oh, yes, he died, all right. He wouldn't have a tomb if he hadn't died. No, it was the *way* he died. *He had no choice about it.*"

"You mean—?"

Jim looked at her and spoke gravely: "Snip-Hotep will always be remembered as the man who gave Queen Nefertari a scrunch perm, and who never lived to see it grow out."

"Erk!"

"The Queen was furious. She'd fallen asleep on the Royal Salon Coiffure Seat and when she woke … well, that was the end of Snip-Hotep."

"Talk about a bad hair day," Doris squawked.

"Apparently, after the Royal Guards put Snip-Hotep to death, the Queen suffered great remorse. Some said her heart almost stopped beating from aching so much. She missed him terribly, and there was no

one else who could give her a set and rinse the way he could."

"Rark!"

"She ordered that he be given a grand burial, with this lavish tomb built especially. Up until now, of course, we've only known about it from a few papyrus accounts, but here" – he swept the lantern beam all around the walls – "is the proof!"

From behind them, far up at the top of the narrow passage they had descended to enter the tomb, came an inquiring snort, gentle yet concerned.

"Quaaaaaaaaooooooo?"

"It's okay, Brenda, my lovely," Jim called back over his shoulder. "We're all right."

Up on the ground, Brenda the Wonder Camel heard him. She rolled her huge head and neck, and the hairs in her mane wafted in the hot desert breeze.

"It's a pity Brenda couldn't fit down the passage," Doris prerked. "It feels funny not having her here with us."

"It's probably a good thing," Jim said, returning his gaze to the hieroglyphs. "She can keep watch up there. And if – heaven forbid – anything goes wrong down here, she can get help."

"Wh-wh-what's going to go wrong?" asked Doris. (Even though she had accompanied Jim into many such tombs, being underground or in confined spaces always made her edgy.)

Jim put down the lantern and slung off his knapsack.

"Don't worry, my dear. I'm just being precautionary."

Doris flew off his shoulder and landed next to the knapsack, on the cool, hard floor. She watched as Jim took out his calfskin-bound notebook from one of his shirt pockets and opened it to a blank page.

"How about you start deciphering some of these hieroglyphs?" he suggested. "I'll note them down in my Record Those Ancient Snippets For Posterity Jotter. Maybe we'll even find the directions to Snip-Hotep's sarcophagus chamber."

"Rark. Let's get started. Which wall first?"

"Hmmm." The archaeologist-poet removed the pencil from the jotter's pencil-holder and tapped the point against his chin. "How about that one with the royal scene of Nefertari being crowned Queen?"

"As good a place as any to start," said Doris. She raised her wings and flew across the chamber, landing on the floor about two metres in front of the wall.

Cairo Jim followed her and stood in the centre of the tomb. Beneath his boots was a diamond-shaped floor tile which had an inlaid marble design of a pair of ancient scissors.

He wetted the point of his pencil with his tongue and waited while Doris found a good place in the hieroglyphs to begin her deciphering.

"Let's see," she muttered. "Somewhere there should be a name or something." She blinked, then jerked her neck up and down three times. "Ah! Got it! Ready, Jim?"

"Ready, my dear."

"A-herm. Here goes: 'Herein lies the Royal Hairdresser Snip-Hotep, Master of Braiding, Vizier of Follicles, the Most Accomplished Head-Shaver, Eyelash Tinter and Eyebrow Arranger in all of Thebes, and in all of the lands of Egypt.'"

Jim carefully took down the details.

"'None was greater than he in the Sacred Arts of'—" And there she stopped.

Jim looked up from his jotter. "What is it, Doris? Have the hieroglyphs run out?"

Quickly she turned and blinked at him. "Shhh, Jim! Listen!"

He tilted back his pith helmet and frowned. "What do you hear?"

The macaw raised a wing to quieten him. "Listen," she repeated.

Jim strained to detect what she was hearing. After a moment he spoke. "All I can hear is the wind coming down the passage from the sandhills above."

"No, Jim, there's something else. A sort of…"

Then Cairo Jim's ears became aware. "Swoggle me subterraneously," he murmured.

Doris blinked nervously.

A low rumbling was coming from somewhere underneath them. Slowly, almost unnoticeably, it was growing louder and louder.

A plump bead of perspiration slowly dribbled from under Jim's pith helmet, down his forehead, into his right eyebrow.

13

Doris stayed where she was, motionless. Only her eyes moved back and forth.

Then Doris felt the vibration. Coming through the floor, it spread up into her claws, legs and belly. In less than two seconds, all her feathers were ajudder.

"Reerraaaaark!" she screeched, lifting her wings and flying upwards to a shelf in the rock wall. She landed on it and called down to Jim. "The floor!"

The vibrations had risen up into Jim, too: up through his sturdy boots and strong kneecaps; up through his legs and stomach; all the way up to the top of his skull.

"Those ancient Egyptians," he shouted to Doris. "Another example of their incredible—"

There he stopped, for what happened at that moment filled his shaking body with a deep, gut-clenching dread.

Swiftly, grittily, the floor all around the diamond-shaped tile on which he was standing began to lower. Down, down, down it went as the vibrations grew stronger and more frenzied.

"Jim!" Doris screeched. "What in the great wide cosmos is *this*?"

"It must be to do with Snip-Hotep," he called back, watching the floor descend further and further. "He must've been considered powerful, even after his death. The tomb builders set all this up to keep people away from what's in here!"

The floor continued to descend, moving further

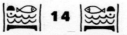

14

away from Jim, leaving him stranded on his tile high atop a single column of stone.

Down

    Down

        Down shuddered the floor, into the gloomy destiny designed by the ancient tomb builders.

Clouds of dust rose into the chamber, billowing all around Jim and Doris.

Jim leant over the edge of his diamond-shaped tile and peered down, shining his torch through the dust below. He was careful not to overbalance or get too close to the edge: the tile was little wider than his shoulders, and there was not much room for him to move in any direction.

Nearly ten metres below him the torchbeam picked out his knapsack sitting alone on the retreating floor, abandoned and so far away.

"Scraaaark! Jim, it's slowing!"

"So it is." He put his jotter in his pocket and listened as the gravelly crunching came to a stop, and the floor did likewise.

Jim could feel the back of his shirt awash with sweat. He suddenly realised how high above the floor he was, and a wave of light-headedness swept over him. He teetered backwards, the heel of his boot slipping over the edge of the tile.

"Jim! TAKE A DEEP BREATH!"

Doris's loudness pierced his brain, and he immediately did as she'd told him. The dusty air filled

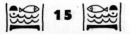

his lungs; he straightened his spine and moved back to the centre of the tile.

"Thank you, my dear," he whispered. "I-I-I don't much care for heights."

Doris looked across at her stranded friend. She knew that the thing to do now was to get him and herself out of this place. That was the most important priority. The tomb of Snip-Hotep could wait.

She raised her wings and swooped down to land gently on his damp shoulder.

"Listen, I've got a plan to get you out of here," she announced in her now-listen-and-don't-say-a-word-until-I've-finished sort of voice.

Jim held out his arm and she waddled down towards his elbow so that he could see her as she was speaking.

"I'll fly over to the passage we came in by. I'll get Brenda to lower a rope down the passage, and I'll fly the end of the rope over to you. You'll tie it around your middle, under your arms, and then I'll give the signal to Brenda to pull you off this tile and up through the passage. Got it?"

"Got it," Jim answered. "Only there's one small problem."

"What?" Doris blinked impatiently. "I'm a bird of action, I don't have time for details!"

"Look," said Jim.

He extended his arm further out and turned slightly (being mindful to keep his balance), so that Doris was facing the passage.

Her beak fell. "Oh," she muttered with a mixture of great annoyance and even greater disappointment.

The passage had filled with rubble: rocks and sand and big pieces of old, dark wooden beams. There was no space between all the debris for the macaw to squeeze through and fly up to Brenda.

"So what do we do?" Doris asked in a small voice.

Jim's heart was beating urgently, pumpapumpa-pumpapumpa, hard against his shirt. "Now don't worry, Doris," he tried to reassure her. "I'm sure Brenda felt all those vibrations ... she's an extremely sensitive camel, as we've come to learn. Why, I bet that right now she's got her snout in all that rubbish, and she's clearing the passage as though there's no tomorrow."

"I wish," said Doris with a small gulp, "you hadn't put it quite like *that*."

"Just a figure of speech, my dear. Just a—"

"Oh, no!" A movement on the walls had caught her eye. She spun her head around. "One, two, three, four! What ... what are they, Jim?"

The archaeologist-poet swivelled his gaze all about. There, on each of the four walls, six previously concealed openings in the hieroglyph-covered plaster had silently appeared.

Each of these twenty-four openings was placed at exactly the same height as Cairo Jim's diamond-shaped tile, and emerging stealthily from each of the openings was a long, sharp, gleaming, spear.

"J ... Jim?"

"I … I don't know, Doris. I've never seen anything like them in any other tombs!"

The twenty-four spears continued to emerge, horizontally and quietly, into the chamber. Then, when each of them was five metres away from Jim and Doris, they stopped.

"One thing's clear," Jim muttered. "It's some sort of Exploration Deterrent. No doubt about it."

"I wish we were in Acapulco," Doris whispered, her feathers standing on end.

Each spear point was aimed at the spot where Jim, with Doris on his arm, was trapped. There was no question about it: whatever was on that diamond-shaped tile was meant to be their target.

His mind reeled with panic – the hollow, dire panic of uncertainty. What had the ancient architects of this tomb designed these spears to do? Would they suddenly lunge inwards? How long would they remain suspended like this? And if they *did* lunge, would they be slow, or razor-sharp, slicing through the air and—?

Five seconds later, Time provided an answer.

There was a quiet clicking from each of the twenty-four openings. Then, with a screeching of ancient iron, the points on each of the spears separated into two.

Doris slapped a wing across the feathers on the top of her head. "They're … they're … "

"Scissors!" exclaimed Jim. "Ancient gigantic iron scissors!"

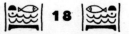

Each pair of scissors was opening slowly. Half of them were set up so that their gleaming, sharp blades were horizontal and level with the floor, far far below, while the others had been positioned so that their blades were vertical and level with the walls.

No matter how they were arranged, it was obvious to Jim that if the scissors moved forwards they would slice anything in their path to ribbons!

Now, all of the scissor-blades were fully opened. "They're enormous," Jim muttered. The distance between each pair of blades was nearly two metres, and Jim noticed, through his rising terror, that there was a hole near the point of each blade. He nodded as he remembered that ancient Egyptian scissors from the 19th Dynasty always had these holes in their blades for some mysterious reason.

"I need all of this like beak ache," Doris squawked.

The next movement came from the giant scissors that were horizontal: in the blink of an eye, they sliced through the air, their blades snapping fiercely and resoundingly shut.

Zing!

The sound speared and echoed into the tomb. ZING! ZING! ZING! ZING! ZING! ZING! ZING! ZING! ZING! ZING! ZING!

Then the vertically placed scissors snapped shut, their sounds even louder than the first group.

ZING! ZING! ZING! ZING! ZING! ZING! ZING! ZING! ZING! ZING! ZING! ZING!

Quickly the blades opened again. Even more quickly they snapped shut, their pointed ends glinting as Jim's torchbeam swung all around.

ZING! ZING! ZING! ZING! ZING! ZING! ZING! ZING! ZING! ZING! ZING! ZING!

"The noise!" shrieked Doris. "Deafening!"

ZING! ZING! ZING! ZING! ZING! ZING! ZING! ZING! ZING! ZING! ZING! ZING!

As the sounds sliced through the musty air, the blades continued opening and closing. ZING! Some opened fast – ZING! Others less so – ZING! All of them – ZING!—seemed unstoppable.

And then, as they kept opening – ZING! – and closing – ZING! – they started the final phase of their menace: moving inwards!

"They're coming at us, Doris! They're on their way!"

"SCRAAAAAAAARK!"

Cairo Jim crouched down on the diamond-shaped tile, hoping to avoid the blades. Steadily, second by second – ZING! ZING! ZING! ZING! ZING! ZING! ZING! – they were getting nearer and nearer.

He flashed his light all around, and realised that even crouching, there was no way to avoid the horizontal scissors.

Moment by razor-sharp moment, the blades were encroaching. Four metres away.

ZING!

Three metres!

ZING!

Two metres, and moving faster, wilder, sharper!

ZING! ZING! ZING! ZING! ZING! ZING! ZING!

He took a huge breath and looked down.

ZING! ZING! ZING! ZING! ZING! ZING! ZING!
ZING! ZING!

"Raaark! Don't Jim! If you jump all that way, you'll break your neck!"

ZING! ZING! ZING! ZING! ZING! ZING! ZING!
ZING! ZING! ZING! ZING! ZING!

"Doris! My dear, fly away from me! Fly down there, or up, out of the path of the blades!"

"Don't be ridiculous!" She wrapped a wing around his neck. "We're together always, no matter what!"

"No, fly! At least you'll be saved!"

His torchbeam flailed wildly about, so far below, so high above, glinting and sparking off the sharpness all around...

ZING! ZING! ZING! ZING! ZING! ZING! ZING!
ZING! ZING! ZING! ZING! ZING!

The gleam from his torch bounced off all of the blades and then, in a twinkling, lit up something in his memory: "Doris!" he shouted, "I have an idea!"

2

YOU NEVER KNOW...

JOCELYN OSGOOD, Chief Flight Attendant with Valkyrian Airways and Cairo Jim's 'good friend', uncrossed her jodhpurred legs and leant forward on her camp stool. "So what did you do, Jim? How did you—?"

"Now there," piped up Doris, sitting on her mahogany perch next to the camp table where Jocelyn and Jim were sipping strong Egyptian tea in the warm afternoon breeze, "is another example of Jim's ingenuity in the face of awfulness. Rark!"

"Quaaaooo!" snorted Brenda the Wonder Camel, relaxing on her sandcarpet between Jim and his much-patched tent. She raised her head from her newest Western adventure novel – *Melodious Tex and the Tumbleweeds of Terror* – and listened attentively to Jim's story ... even though she had heard Doris and Jim tell it before, she still delighted in the outcome.

Jocelyn ran a hand through her tangly auburn curls, and took off her sun-spectacles. "Will you *please* tell me?" she demanded, her eyes blazing with urgency and worry. "What did you do?"

"Well," said Jim. He put down his cup and saucer and smiled fondly at her (Doris saw this and gave a

sharp screech, which no one took any notice of). "As the blades were closing in on me, I suddenly – and fortuitously – remembered one of the mottos of the Old Relics Society."

Jocelyn looked puzzled. "'Never Put Your Hairbrush Down Next to a Porcupine'?" she asked.

"No, not that one. The *main* motto."

Doris puffed out her chestfeathers and declaimed, "'You Never Know When You'll Need A Good Bit of String.'"

"Ah." Jocelyn nodded, waiting for more.

"Yes," said Jim, nodding back.

"Rark," rarked Doris, nodding also.

"Quaaaaaooo," Brenda snorted, nodding her head in a rolling motion and swishing her tail against her sandcarpet.

Jocelyn dug her fingernails into the kneecap pads on her jodhpurs. *"So what happened when you'd remembered this?"*

"Oh," said Cairo Jim. "Then I remembered something else. Gerald Perry* had just sent down his February package. We got it the day before we went in to Snip-Hotep's tomb."

Brenda arched her neck back and sent out a thought. "He always sends one down, on February 15th. As regularly as patchwork, our friend Mrs Amun-Ra says."

---

* Gerald Perry Esquire, Cairo Jim's patron and the Founder of the Old Relics Society in Cairo

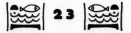

Doris opened and closed her wings as Brenda's thought permeated her feathers. "He always sends one down, on February 15th," she squawked. "As regularly as patchwork, our friend Mrs Amun-Ra says."

"And this package always has the same thing in it," said Jim.

"*What?*" demanded Jocelyn, her fingernails scrunching her kneepads.

"A good bit of string, of course," answered Doris, blinking at her.

"His February package," mused Jim. "Why, I've had so much string over all the Februaries that, if I'd wanted to, I could've tied it all together and it probably would've stretched from here to the pyramids up in Giza, and I could've wound it around the Great Pyramid a hundred times, or maybe two hundred times, and there'd still be some of the string left in my hand." He paused and thought for a moment. "Not that I've ever wanted to do that, of course."

Jocelyn scratched the curls on the back of her head. "Jim, please! What's a package with a good bit of string in it got to do with *February*? And how did that help you?"

"You tell her, Doris."

"Quaaaoooo," agreed Brenda.

The macaw cleared her throat and spoke clearly:

"'Thirty days hath September,
April, June and November.
All the rest have thirty-one,

24

excepting for February alone, so you need
a Good Bit of String from the Old Relics Society.'"

"Yes," said Jim. "Everyone knows that. And it was extremely lucky for us that Perry had decided, this year, to send to all the Society Members a revolutionary new type of string, recently discovered in the hinterland regions of Western Sulawesi." He picked up his cup and had a sip of his tea.

"Jim! Don't stop!"

"You see, Joss, this string is unlike any other sort of string ever found. It's very fine – not much thicker than a hair – but *strong*."

"Rark! It's stronger than ten thousand bits of string fused together!" Doris squawked, jerking up and down on her perch.

"But there's more to it than that," thought Brenda, swishing her tail against a pesky fly.

"But there's more to it than that," Jim continued. "You see, this string from Western Sulawesi also has a special property that no other string known to man, woman, macaw or Wonder Camel possesses. When it is pulled, it emits water!"

"Water?" Jocelyn repeated. "I've never heard of such a thing."

"No, neither had we, until Perry sent us a coil of it. The tauter the string gets, the wetter it becomes. When the string isn't being pulled, it's as dry as a hyena's tail in the desert sun."

Jocelyn put her sun-spectacles back on and looked impressed (and a tad astounded).

"We call it the Stringy, Quiet, Ultra Elastic, Lightweight, Convenient, Hardy Excavational Rescuer," Jim said.

"The SQUELCHER," added Doris.

"Do you have it here?"

"No, unfortunately not," answered Jim. "We had to leave it all down in Snip-Hotep's tomb. That's how we escaped, you see."

"Rark." Doris blinked. "Jim had the bright idea that I fly down to his knapsack and get out this ball of string."

"You see, Joss, I'd noticed that each of the ancient scissor blades had a small hole just near the point."

"Quaaaooo," Brenda snorted. For her, this was the best part of the story.

"So Doris flew up with the SQUELCHER, which was still dry, of course. She gave me one end of the ball and then, as the scissors bore closer—"

"Zing! Zing! Zing!" screeched the macaw, causing everyone to jump.

"—and being careful not to get an unwanted trim, Doris darted in between them, around each point and sometimes straight between two blades just as they opened, threading her end of the SQUELCHER through the holes. As soon as the end of the SQUELCHER was threaded through a pair of blades, she gave it a good yank with her beak."

"Once I'd threaded one pair of scissors," Doris added, "I'd fly to the next pair and thread that. And then on to the next one, and—"

"But," Jocelyn interrupted, "surely the scissors would've been too strong? Didn't they cut through the string, or snap it when their blades opened?"

"Ah." Jim smiled. "You're right, Joss. That *would've* happened, had not Doris been stretching it. You see, no sooner was the SQUELCHER pulled tight through each hole, than a large splurting of water poured forth, all down the blades to the fulcrum. Being so ancient, and not having had any contact with fresh air or moisture for thousands of years, well, every pair of scissors—"

"Rusted!" exclaimed Jocelyn.

"Rusted and busted!" squawked Doris.

Jim nodded. "They rusted in a matter of seconds, shutting down completely. And, as I'd hoped, the mechanism driving them forward, towards me, couldn't cope with the sudden stopping of the blades. The scissors ground to a halt, some half-opened, some closed, and didn't move a millimetre. You should've heard it, Joss … each pair of scissors sounded like it was groaning in awful agony as it seized up!"

"They 'heaved forth such groans, that their discharge did stretch … almost to bursting'!" quoted Doris from *As You Like It* by William Shakespeare.

Despite the heat of the desert, Jocelyn shuddered.

"By the time Doris threaded the last pair, she was

 **27**

just in time – the tips of one particular pair of scissors were about to slice through the pockets on the back of my shorts, and that would've been the beginnings of disaster – I use those pockets to keep all sorts of small but necessary things in."

"And it's always good to be able to sit down properly," thought Brenda.

"And," said Doris (picking up the Wonder Camel's thought, but not realising that she had), "it's always good to be able to sit down properly. Rark."

"Then what happened?" asked Jocelyn.

"By then," Jim told her, "Brenda had managed to dislodge some of the fallen beams and rocks from the entrance of the passage."

"Strong, beautiful Brenda," commented Jocelyn, flashing a big smile at Brenda.

"Quaaaaoo." Brenda fluttered her long eyelashes in an all-part-of-the-job sort of way.

"Then," continued Jim, "Doris flew up the passage and back here to camp, where she found our coil of long rope. She brought that back to Brenda—"

"Quaaaaaoo!"

"—who had made a big enough opening in the passageway for me to get through. Doris tied one end of the rope around Brenda's middle, and flew down the passageway with the other end in her beak. This end I tied around *my* middle."

Doris took up the story. "Then Brenda dug her hoofs

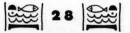

28

into the sands above. Jim stepped off the diamond-shaped tile—"

"I hope I never have to do anything like *that* again," muttered the archaeologist-poet.

"—and he swung back and forth, like a big pendulum, trying not to bump against the rusted scissors, while Brenda and I slowly hauled him up and into the passage. I hovered near him throughout, making sure he was coping and not suffering any great discomfort." Doris had added that last bit proudly and (thought Jocelyn) a little protectively.

"And soon, Jim concluded, "we were, all three of us, together again, on the hot sands above."

"Daylight at last," cooed Doris, and Brenda rolled her head in a wide circle.

Jocelyn's heart was beating hard against her blouse. "What a team you are! I know you've been in some dangerous scrapes before, but this had to be one of the worst."

"Rark. We'll look for ancientness 'even in the jaws of danger and of death'," quoted Doris.

"Very good, my dear," said Jim.

"Quaaaooo," agreed Brenda.

Doris hop-fluttered from her perch and landed on the top of Cairo Jim's pith helmet. She waddled down onto his shoulder. "*King John* by Mr Shakespeare. Act Five, Scene Two."

"You poetic macaw," said Jocelyn, reaching across and tousling Doris's wingfeathers.

 **29**

"*Reeeeeraaaaark!*"

Quickly Jocelyn withdrew her hand and, just as quickly, Doris flew back to her mahogany perch.

Then, like a gunshot in the still desert air, the sudden slamming of a car door made all four of them start and turn.

Jim stood and squinted through his special desert sun-spectacles. Above the camp, on the road tucked between the sandhills, he saw a car: a dark green vintage Bentley. An elderly figure dressed in a cream linen suit and large-brimmed fedora was walking slowly away from the car, towards the camp.

"And stay in there, Garth," the old man was saying over his shoulder, to someone inside the car. "Wait for me till I come back. You always seem to attract donkeys whenever y'come down here!"

"It's Perry," Jim announced, going to meet his patron.

"Perry," repeated Doris, flexing herself up and down on her perch.

"Long time no see," said Jocelyn Osgood.

Brenda the Wonder Camel watched as Gerald Perry Esquire approached the camp. She snorted quietly, closed *Melodious Tex and the Tumbleweeds of Terror* with her snout, flicked a few flies from her rear hump with her tail, and thought that something was wrong: Gerald Perry never visited their campsite unannounced unless there was trouble.

MILLICENT SPULE
IS ALARMED!

CAIRO JIM tilted his pith helmet back off his forehead and extended his hand. "Perry! Good to see you!"

The elderly, possum-faced gentleman looked up at his favourite archaeologist and one of the most popular members of the Old Relics Society. "Jim!" He shook Jim's hand firmly yet fondly. "Likewise, m'boy, likewise."

"How are you?" Jim guided Perry down the sandhill towards the campsite.

"Oh, a bit under the weather, if y'really want to know. Last night we had the Society's annual fancy-dress evening."

"Yes, I'm sorry I missed it," said Jim, even though he had never intended to go.

"Oh, y'would've enjoyed it, Jim. This year the theme was 'Our Four-legged Friends'. It was a fun evening, but very exhausting. I went as a Serengeti zebra – never again, the hoofs chafed m'ankles *dreadfully*! Clive Skeggs came as a giraffe, until his head and neck fell off into the punch bowl."

"Oh dear."

"Yes, I don't think he meant *that* t'happen. And old Esmond Horneplush dressed up as Bambi. He still

can't stand up straight, poor fellow, but he *has* found a lot of lost coins on the floor and in the hallways. Antonio Horgan was an antelope, complete with Styrofoam antlers, and Spong, the receptionist – you remember him, Jim, very nervous sort of chap—"

"Yes," said Jim.

"—well, he got kitted out as a centaur. Never knew that Spong was such a *hairy* man, but never mind about that. And you should've seen Anthea Martin, our early Hittite historian. She came disguised as a woolly little baby sheep, but it wasn't a very good costume. We could all tell it was Martin dressed as lamb."

Jim and Perry had by this time arrived at the campsite.

"Rark! Greetings and salutations!" screeched Doris.

"Quaaaaoooo!" welcomed Brenda.

Jocelyn went over to Perry and gave him a friendly kiss on the cheek. "Hello, Mr Perry."

Gerald Perry blushed momentarily and rubbed his moustache this way and that. "Joss! Please, y'must call me Gerald. Any 'good friend' of Jim's is hopefully a 'good friend' of mine." He wiggled his eyebrows and pumped her hand vigorously.

"Lovely to see you again, Gerald," Jocelyn said.

"Here we are," said Jim, offering Perry his camp chair.

"Thank you, m'boy." The elderly man sat and took off his fedora, which he used to fan his face.

"I'll just get you some cool water," offered Jim, but Perry held up his hand and spoke in a subdued, solemn tone.

 32

"That can wait, Jim. What I've got to tell you is much more urgent than liquid refreshments, cool or otherwise..."

As Gerald Perry Esquire was declining Jim's offer of a cool glass of water, up on the Greek island of Crete, at the ancient site of the Palace of Knossos, a drifting obnoxiousness was spreading all around.

It had begun – as it had begun every morning for the last month – with a faint but irking-the-sides-of-the-nostrils odour. This odour was stale and strange, and if you were to linger while it filled the air around you, it would soon infiltrate your nasal passages and creep downwards, into your throat.

From there it would spread further – you would be tasting it by this time, somewhere on the back of your tongue. Soon the air around you would be filled completely with the odour, and you'd wonder just what the stench might have come from.

It's sweetish, you would think, trying to gulp the disgusting taste away. *Too* sweetish.

Sweetish to the point of rottenness.

Vile and putrid.

And then, just as you realise you can't stay here a minute longer without being violently sick, you realise what the stink might once have been: *prunes*. Rotting prunes, liquefying and turning into this wretched gas, the likes of which you have never smelt before. And you hope you will never smell again.

 **33**

You would also feel, around about this time, your skin erupting with the most awful itchiness. As though boiling water was seeping under the surface, prickling the pores all over you.

At this point you would flee – hurrying from the Palace of Knossos, holding your breath for as long as you could.

But, having fled, you would not see that which always emerged when the putrid gas was at its thickest. You would miss the sight which, at this moment, while Gerald Perry back in Egypt was recounting his tale to his friends, has arrived on the scene.

A large, obese figure, clad in a tight-fitting rubber suit with two oxygen cylinders on its back, its face covered by a bulging gas mask, and with a sometimes-flapping rubber-covered creature on its shoulder (whose upper-most parts are covered by an old, stained handkerchief), strides undaunted through the swirling rottenness.

And disappears silently into the ground.

"Prune-smelling gases?" asked Cairo Jim, sitting next to Brenda on her sandcarpet in front of Perry's chair.

"Erk," erked Doris.

"According to Millicent Spule," said Perry.

"Millicent Spule," said Jim, smiling warmly.

Jocelyn crossed her jodhpurred legs the other way. "And who, may I ask, is Millicent Spule?"

"Mmm?" Jim, who had been thinking back to his Archaeology School days, blinked and transferred his

smile to Jocelyn. "Oh, Millicent Spule was a friend of mine when I was studying. She's very … enthusiastic."

"That's one way of putting it," Perry added, winking at Jim.

"I see," said Jocelyn, raising an eyebrow.

Perry said, "She's gone on to become an expert on early Minoan letter-seals and toenail ornamentation methods."

"She studies *ancient nail polish*?" Jocelyn asked, with a small sniff.

"Er, well, yes," stammered Perry. "But she knows more about it than any other soul on the planet."

"She always clears her throat very loudly whenever she speaks," thought Brenda, who had met Millicent Spule once on a trip to Cairo with Jim and Doris.

"She always clears her throat very loudly whenever she speaks," added Perry, although he wasn't quite sure why he was telling this bit of information to Jocelyn. It must have just popped into his head for some reason, he decided.

"Yes," added Jim. "Sounds like she's firing a machine-gun at you from her tonsils, but you soon get used to it."

"Anyway," Perry said, "she's just come back from Knossos, and this morning she burst into the library at the Old Relics Society and told me all about this strange stench."

"Prunes," Doris muttered, thinking hard.

Perry dabbed at the back of his neck with an osnaburg handkerchief. "Millicent first encountered the

 **3 5**

strange gas a week ago … she was back at Knossos on her routine visit, trying to unearth samples of Minoan nail polish. The awful smell drove her from the ruins, along with the handful of tourists who were at the site at the same time."

"So it's widespread," said Jim, clasping his hands around his kneecaps. "All sorts of people are affected by it."

"Oh, yes." Perry's eyes were wide. "Millicent went into the town afterwards to ask the local folk all about the gases. Apparently, anyone who visits the site – archaeologists and holidaying visitors, souvenir vendors or hot-food sellers – can't stand it. Everyone skedaddles, faster than a papyrus seller running after a bunch of tourists."

"Hmmm." Cairo Jim started visualising the scene. "So the site becomes deserted very quickly."

"Completely deserted," Perry answered. "The townsfolk told Millicent that no one can stand to be there while the gases are lurking. At the beginning one man tried to hang around, but he got such a severe headache he had to stay in bed with a wet flannel on his head for three whole days. And his skin broke out in the most fierce rash!"

"How long has this been happening?" asked Doris, opening and closing her wings.

"Millicent was told that the gases have been going on for a month. Starts at the same time every morning: ten o'clock."

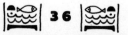

"Which," pondered Jim, "if my memory serves me correctly, is the time the Palace opens to the public."

"That's right, m'boy. The very hour!"

Jocelyn leant forward. "Maybe," she suggested, "the gas is escaping from geological fault lines deep underground? Maybe these fault lines go all the way to some rivers or springs somewhere in the surrounding hillsides, and the smell is travelling all that distance and coming up through some cracks at the Knossos ruins?"

Jim, Brenda and Doris listened, as did Perry (who was also slightly dazzled by Jocelyn's lustrous auburn curls … he hadn't seen her for some time, and had forgotten how abundant they were).

"It's possible," Jocelyn went on. "Remember what those archaeologists discovered up at Delphi? They found fault lines and fissures directly under the ancient Temple of the Oracle, which led off to old water sources. They reckoned that the famous oracle – she who could see into the future and foretell all manner of things to come – was actually suffering from gaseous emissions."

"Ergh!" said Perry.

"That's right," Doris chirped. "Ethylene and ethane and methane and other nasty stuff!"

"It's a possibility," considered Brenda, flaring her nostrils thoughtfully.

"It's a possibility," said Jim. "But if that *was* the case, why would it smell of *prunes*?"

Jocelyn asked Perry, "Did Millicent Spule find out how long these gaseous intrusions lasted?"

"She did, she did. The local folk told her that after about seven hours, the last of the stench had disappeared. By that time, of course, the site was closed for the day to visitors."

"Odder and odder," squawked Doris, shaking her beak.

"The locals also told her that some of them have thought they've seen a figure emerging, then *disappearing*. Seems that this figure gets swallowed up by the ground!"

"A figure?" Jim asked, his eyebrows furrowing.

"Mmm," nodded Perry. "But Millicent couldn't get any more out of 'em – it seems the folk up there don't like to talk about strange goings-on too much."

"So," said Jocelyn, "apart from this mysterious figure, no one has really been able to visit the ruins for the last month?"

"That's right," answered the elderly gentleman. "Except for Millicent Spule."

"But you said—"

"Ah!" Perry's eyes twinkled. "She's resourceful, is Millicent. She decided, with the aid of a key she borrowed from a member of the Greek Antiquities Squad, that she wasn't going to be denied her visit to her favourite archaeological site. No, siree. So a few nights ago she opened the entrance gates under cover of moonlight, and crept into the grounds. She spent the whole night pottering around the Palace."

"Looking for her ancient nail polish," Jocelyn said.

"Well, yes and no. Y'see, at first she started sniffing about for that sort of thing, but after an hour or so she found that she had got quite angry. She said she felt outraged that she'd been stopped from spending her time pursuing her occupation. So she started looking instead for any clues as to where this awful, disruptive smell was emanating from."

"And did she find where?" asked Jim.

"Well, yes again, and no again."

"Rark. I don't understand!"

Gerald Perry reached into his coat pocket and brought out a small object wrapped in lavender-coloured tissue paper and tied with a thin piece of burgundy-coloured ribbon. "She found this," he told everyone, his voice low and troubled.

Jim, Brenda, Doris and Jocelyn watched as Perry laid the small package on his knees and untied the ribbon. "I had Spong at the Society wrap it for me before I left," he muttered as he pocketed the ribbon and unwrapped the tissue paper.

When the paper was off, everyone saw what had been concealed: a slender, silver object with a gilt handle.

Jocelyn frowned. "A ... a nailfile?"

Already, Jim's blood had started to chill, and Doris and Brenda's heartbeats quickened.

"Exactly," said Perry. He handed the file over to her. "Read the brand name, down there on the lower part of the handle, near the bottom edge."

The Flight Attendant lifted her sun-spectacles and peered at the small engraved name. "Hmm. 'Fingertips of Subtlety™'."

"Is it of interest?" asked Jim.

"One of the best brands on the market, according to my friend Joan Twilight."★

"Turn it over," said Perry.

Jocelyn did so. There, on the reverse side of the handle, in a flowing and grandiose script, was an engraving: three letters and an inscription.

"'*N.F.B.*'," Jocelyn read aloud. "'*With endless oceans of love from your adoring Mumsy Wumsy.*'"

Doris's feathers went haywire. "Raaaaaaaaaaark! Reeeeeeraaaaaaaark! Not him!"

And Brenda's humps tingled with dread.

It was Jim who said the name: "Bone!"

"Neptune Flannelbottom Bone," Perry confirmed. "The dreadful brute himself."

"That cowardly, greedy, selfish, egomaniac," Brenda thought, seething quietly. "That worst-dressed archaeologist in the history of the profession."

"That cowardly, greedy, selfish, egomaniac," Jocelyn said, dropping the nailfile disdainfully onto the sand. "That worst-dressed archaeologist in the history of your profession."

"The man," Perry added, "who's tried to dupe and

★ Jocelyn's former colleague and Probationary Flight Attendant with Valkyrian Airways

 40

swindle you, Cairo Jim, out of every discovery you and Doris and Brenda've ever made."

Jim stood, his legs not as sturdy as they had been a few minutes ago. He looked out at the sand dunes, at the dark shadows falling slowly across the ridges with the setting sun, and as he did so, the overblown, colossal image of Neptune Bone and his gruesome raven, Desdemona, filled the shadows of his memory.

Then, in the dancing of a sand grain across the desert, the poetry cells in his brain were infused with that memory, and he found himself blurting a poem:

> "From Snip-Hotep we have survived
> thanks to Perry's SQUELCHER,
> but now a new threat is revived
> – Neptune Bone's returned and thrived
> – with stabbing force our peace he's knived,
> with his raven belcher!"

Gerald Perry shuddered at Jim's outburst. "This is no time for poetry, Jim."

Jocelyn pulled a strange face as though she had just swallowed castor oil. Fond as she was of her archaeologist-poet friend, she did not especially care for his poems.

Doris rolled her small eyes, and the feathers around the edges of her beak crinkled with slight distaste.

(Only Brenda gave an appreciative snort – she always enjoyed this side to Cairo Jim.)

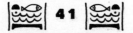 41

"But," squawked Doris, "we thought we'd seen the last of Bone, back at the Colosseum in Italy!"*

"It seems not," Perry said. "It seems he's resurfaced, up at the palace of Knossos, with all this vile gas."

"That's Bone, all right," Doris said. "Vile gas personified!"

"Of course!" exclaimed Jim. "The prunes! That explains it. Bone's always had a predilection for prunes. Prunes and those ghastly cigars he smokes."

"And manicuring his fingernails to the point of obsession," Doris added.

Then a thought hit Jim like a rubber glove filled with jelly, and his spine tingled with urgency and fear. "He's ... he's going *underground*," he whispered.

Perry nodded. "That's what the locals told Millicent Spule."

Jim whipped off his special desert sun-spectacles and faced his friends. His eyes were shining with concern. "Do you think it's possible ... oh, no, it can't be..."

"What, Jim?" asked Jocelyn, going to his side.

"Rark!" Doris flew off her perch and came to land on Jim's shoulder, in between him and Jocelyn Osgood. "What might be possible?" she screeched.

"Go on, Jim," said Perry.

"Quaaaaoo," snorted Brenda, who had something of an idea what he might say.

---

* See *Cairo Jim and the Tyrannical Bauble of Tiberius – A Tale of Ancient Atrocity*

"Well," Jim said, "do you think that Bone – that vile usurper, we know he is, but we also know that he does tread on the borders of genius every now and then – do you think that he might be looking for the legendary Labyrinth of King Minos?"

Perry sprang out of his chair, his moustache standing on end. "Discombobulations! Of course! They reckon it was built right under the Palace of Knossos!"

"The Labyrinth?" breathed Jocelyn, scarcely able to let herself comprehend the possibility.

Brenda's humps tingled wildly now – this was an astonishing turn.

Doris, who had not read or heard of the Labyrinth of King Minos (despite being a very well-read and highly informed macaw when it comes to archaeology and ancient legends), was in the dark. "Labyrinth? What Labyrinth?"

Jim patted her wing. "I'll tell you and Brenda all about it when we're on our way. Right now there's no time to waste." He turned to his patron. "Perry, with your help I think we should get to Crete immediately. If Bone *is* sniffing around, looking for the Labyrinth, there's no telling what sort of vandalism or worse he'll get up to while trying to find it."

Gerald Perry smiled. "I had a hunch you'd want to go fairly quickly," he said. "It's already arranged. I've got one of m'small aeroplanes coming to collect you and Doris and Brenda in about twenty minutes." He turned to Jocelyn. "And you, Jocelyn, if you'd like to join them."

"Rark!" rarked Doris, flapping her wings. "Maybe Jocelyn Osgood has other things to do? A Flight Attendant's life – especially a *Senior* Flight Attendant's – can be very busy, yes?"

Jocelyn felt a big lump rise in her throat. "Gerald, there's nothing I'd enjoy more than to go with Jim and Doris and Brenda. But unfortunately I can't. This is the last day of my leave, and first thing tomorrow I have to fly with Valkyrian Airways to Jaipur. I'm doing Indian hops for the next month or so."

(Perry looked hopeful for a moment, as he speculated that perhaps this was a new sort of dance which he had not yet tried.)

"What a great pity," said Jim, noticing Jocelyn's intense disappointment.

"Never mind," Perry said. "There'll be lots of other expeditions, I'm sure of that."

"Yes." Jocelyn smiled, and Jim smiled back at her – a smile that she knew meant that there *would* be other expeditions with her 'good friend'.

"Now," the elderly man instructed, "in the plane you'll find oxygen masks and protective suits for the three of you. I had old Teddy Snorkel customise the protective suits you used when you went on that diving expedition in the Red Sea a short while ago."★

"Thank you, Perry, you're always prepared."

★ See *Cairo Jim and the Sunken Sarcophagus of Sekheret – A Tale of Mayhem, Mystery and Moisture*

"Eh? Oh, one has t'be, I've come to find. Otherwise you end up wearing your trousers back-to-front, and that can be very inconvenient. And Brenda, I had the pilots take out the last two rows of seats, so you shouldn't have too much of a squeeze."

"Quaaaaaooo," snorted the Wonder Camel gratefully.

"And, as usual, I've put enough supplies in the plane to last you all for a few days… Malawian snails for you, Doris—"

"Thank you," said the macaw.

"——and special freeze-dried worms for you, Brenda … y'just add water and they taste as fresh as the day they first squirmed, or so I'm told—"

"Quaaaooo."

"—and there's some tinned supplies for you, too, Jim. Some new delicacies I came across recently … rather exotic. I'm sure you'll enjoy 'em. Here's some funds, too, so you won't be out of pocket."

He handed Cairo Jim a wallet, fat with money. The archaeologist-poet accepted it and thanked Perry.

Then, while Doris flew into the tent and got together some 'essential' items she wanted to take, and while Brenda gathered up her Melodious Tex novel and put it inside the tent with all her other Melodious Tex novels, Jim, Jocelyn and Perry waited quietly for the plane to arrive.

With every second that passed, Jim was filling with the same sort of anxiety he always filled with whenever

a new archaeological expedition was before him – especially an expedition involving having to cross paths with Neptune Bone.

All he wanted to do now was to get to the Palace of Knossos and find out exactly what was going on.

◇ ◇ ◇ ◇ ◇ **4** ◇ ◇ ◇ ◇ ◇

RENEGADES IN THE RUBBLE

IT WAS AS IF A HEAVY, invisible curtain of stale prune-stench had draped itself all around the ruins, covering the beautiful red columns and the brightly decorated walls of the Palace, and smothering the very oxygen out of existence.

As the uppermost arc of the sun slowly slid under the crests of the hills surrounding the ruins of Knossos, and as the twilight started to settle in, a deep rumbling rose from under the northern side of the Palace walls.

It sounded as though the earth below was stirring, waking, stretching itself and trying to move.

There was no one about to hear the rumbling ... everyone had long since fled the grounds. Only a few birds, perched high in the trees, were aware of the disturbance.

Then the rumblings changed, becoming more gravelly. Grittier, as though rocks were being shifted against one another.

Gradually the gravel-crunching seemed to rise, approaching the surface of the ground...

...and, slowly, heavily, strainingly, a large slab of marble that was lying on the ground began moving sideways.

"Arrrrrrrrrrr," came a muffled grunt from beneath this slab.

There was a scratching, frantic and teeth-piercing, like something sharp on the underside of the marble.

The marble slab kept shifting, slowly across the ground. Soon it had moved far enough to reveal a hole – a dark place, wide enough for two men to fit into – hewn into the underground rock.

With one last push, and a louder grunt, the slab was pushed clear of the hole.

From this subterranean hiding place, a pair of pudgy, rubber-gloved hands emerged. They gripped the rim of the hole and pressed their palms firmly down on the ground beside the slab.

Up came the owners of those hands, the wide, fleshy body encased in a dull silver rubber suit with two oxygen cylinders on its back, the face covered by a gas mask with a pig-snout breathing aperture at the front. On top of the greasy hair sat a turquoise-coloured fez with a bright orange tassel.

Captain Neptune Flannelbottom Bone swung himself around so that his oversized bottom plonked heavily onto the ground. He panted for a few moments, getting his breath back, then gestured impatiently down into the hole.

"Come on, come on, you lethargic lump of laziness. Get up here and ensure that the air is fit for me to breathe!"

From within the hole, a pair of eyeballs throbbed –

redly, the colour of blood. "Hang onta yer chariot, chubbychops," came a muffled retort.

The silver-suited raven known to Bone and the world as Desdemona flapped her rubber-enclosed wings as she tried to fly out of the hole.

"You dimwitted dollop of dread." Bone scowled beneath his gas mask. "Unharness yourself from the little wagon first."

"Yeah, yeah, yeah." Desdemona stopped flapping and reached around to the back of her neck. Quickly she unclipped the harness that attached the little wagon – the wagon that they used to carry their daily supplies of candles and water and bread rolls and Belch of Brouhaha cigars, which Bone could not live without, and tins of Japanese seaweed, which Desdemona loved.

The harness of the little wagon slumped down, and the raven was unattached. She lifted her wings and flew up to land on the ground next to Bone.

"Well, hurry up. I haven't got all decade. Get your hanky off and sniff."

Desdemona looked at him, her eyes throbbing harder as a nasty thought crept into her mind. Then she pulled the old, stained handkerchief off her beak.

And took in a beakful of air.

"Well?" Bone asked impatiently, as big dollops of sweat ran down his cheeks, through his beard, forming puddlettes in the bottom of his gas mask.

Desdemona screwed up her face-feathers. Her rough yellow tongue came out of her beak and she pointed

the tip of it southwards, from where a small breeze was blowing. "The air's still rancid," she croaked.

"But is it breathable?"

She took another sniff, darted her tongue in and out, and stood on one leg, bringing the other up against her pot-belly. "You'll be right," she told him. "Yer've smelt worse every time you've opened your laundry basket."

Bone lifted his fez, pulled off his gas mask, and threw it at her (she hopped out of the way, as this was not the first time such an exchange had taken place between the two). He plonked the fez back onto his wide head. "You atrocious assortment of acrimony," he sneered, scratching his beard.

"Thank you," she said. "And I just *lervvve* you, too."

He grabbed at the zipper on the front of his rubber suit and yanked it down, towards the base of his enormous belly. The sound of the zipper's teeth travelling across the wide terrain sounded like a whale who had eaten far too many baked beans and was suffering the consequences.

Desdemona unzipped her rubber suit as well, and hopped swiftly out of it.

Bone stood and peeled off the rubber suit and the attached pair of gloves.

With a final grunt, the rubber and the oxygen tanks were around his ankles. He stepped out of the suit and smoothed down his emerald-green waistcoat and his plus-fours trousers, which he had recently ordered from his tailor in Port Moresby and which were decorated

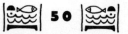

all over with tiny embroidered faces of all the Prime Ministers of Australia. (Bone had not ordered this design; it was the only Crimplene fabric the tailor had available, and nobody else had wanted it.)

Then he took a Belch of Brouhaha cigar from his waistcoat pocket, bit off the end, spat it onto the ground, placed the cigar between his fat lips and lit it.

"Arrrr," he exhaled, blowing the shaft of thick smoke across Desdemona's dull black feathers.

She coughed raspingly and shook her head.

Bone bent over and picked up his crumpled rubber suit and oxygen tanks (the face of Edmund Barton* winked out at Desdemona for an instant, and she cringed).

"Come, bird, back to our lodgings. We need all the rest we can get if we are to start early tomorrow morning. I have a feeling that we are getting closer to that what I am searching for, and tomorrow might be the day we hit the jackpot."

"Haven't you forgotten something?"

"I beg your pardon?" His voice dripped with haughty impatience.

She glared at him, then cocked her beak towards the hole. "Ya haven't covered up the tunnel."

"Arrr. Well observed, birdbrain." He tucked the rubber bundle under his arm and bent over again (Edmund Barton winked once more at the bird, and

---

* The first Prime Minister of Australia

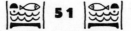

once more she cringed). With great effort Bone pushed the marble slab back across the hole.

"Ugh! There." He dusted down his hands, inspected his precious fingernails, and picked up his gas mask. Puffing self-importantly on the cigar, he turned and strode towards the perimeter fence, and the opening he had cut in it.

"Hey! Crark! Wait for me!" Desdemona kicked her rubberised suit and beak-handkerchief under a rock where they would be hidden until the following morning, and flew after him.

Bone ducked and squeezed under the opening in the wire fence. Desdemona swooped through behind him, and flew around his head and shoulders as he strode towards the heavily wooded foothills.

They passed the three expertly camouflaged forty-gallon drums from where every morning they let loose the prune-stench gases. Then Desdemona's feathers began to stir. In an instant she was besieged by the countless fleas who lived in her dull black plumage.

"Ouch! Youch! Ouch ouch ouchie OUCH!"

"What's up with you?" Bone blew a heavy shaft of smoke at her. "Has a thought tried to penetrate your thick skull again?"

"Very droll. Ha-crark-ha. Nah, it's these confounded fleas. Yowch!"

"If only you'd bathe regularly, they'd leave you well alone."

"Oh, and how could I manage *that* when we're living

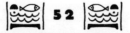

in a dripping cave in the side of that hill up there? That is, when we're not spendin' all our time down below, under that crumblin' Palace, in that underground maze! Sheesh!"

Bone turned a corner in the narrow trail that wound through the dense, darkening bushes. "Stop your grumbling, Desdemona. I admit, our cave in the hill is not the most luxurious of lodgings—"

"It stinks and drips and the wind whips through it like a steam train goin' through tissue paper!"

"—but it is certainly *safe*. Need I remind you that I am still on the wanted lists of thirty-two branches of the Antiquities Squad?"

"Need I remind you that you look ridiculous in those plus-fours? Every time you take a step, James Scullin's cheeks go all wrinkly, and Harold Holt keeps disappearin' in your—"

"Enshut your beak, before I enshut it forcefully! I happen to think these trousers are very tasteful. I bet you won't find another living soul dressed in such elegance as what I am."

"I sincerely hope you're right," she croaked, shuddering at all the small, serious-looking faces dotted across his lower loins.

The path rose more steeply, and Bone started taking bigger strides. Desdemona flew behind him, landing on a bush here and there and watching as he began puffing ahead of her.

"Oh, my Captain?"

"What, you frightful feathered floozie?"

"May I ask a question?"

"Arrrr."

"What exactly are we doin' here? Why have we been spendin' the last four weeks letting off that awful prune smell every mornin' and drivin' those idiot tourists away and then goin' down in them tunnels under the Palace? Day after day, trudgin' through those dark tunnels, gettin' lost, retracin' our tracks. We haven't found a single thing! What's the point of it all? Why? Why? Why?"

"That was six questions, seaweed-breath."

"Crark! One, six, whatsa diff?"

With a big grunt, Bone reached the top of the track. Here, the bushes were thickest, and the track all but dwindled away. Their cave in the hillside was to the right of them, but was undetectable to anyone who didn't know it was there, as it was concealed behind a high, coarse clump of shrubbery and undergrowth.

The hills rose sharply all around, almost straight upwards, encircling this secluded place and closing it off on three sides. On the hillside opposite the concealed cave, a natural spring flowed down the grassy slope, forming a small waterhole among the rocks at the top of the track.

"Well?" rasped Desdemona, fluttering down to land on a branch. "Ya gonna answer me?"

Bone flopped down on a large, moss-covered boulder. He took out his handkerchief and wiped it across the side of the hill, right next to him. The

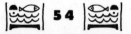

handkerchief soaked up some spring water, and Bone dabbed it earnestly on his face and beard.

"Well? I'm waitin'…" She pecked at a picnic of fleas on her left wing, and spat it onto the ground.

Bone took a big drag on his cigar and blew the smoke down the track. He viewed the scene below, his gaze scanning the tops of the trees, all the way down to the Kephala hill on which were the fenced ruins of Knossos and, past them, to the deserted road that led to the town of Iraklion, five kilometres away.

After a while, his eyes narrowed into slits, and he spoke, his voice low and subdued. "I shall tell you this much for the time being, you querulous quota of queerness. We are here because I have come upon some knowledge that no other living man or woman has ever uncovered."

"Crark. Knowledge?"

"Arrr. A concept with which you have never become acquainted."

"What sorta knowledge?"

"I discovered certain facts, Desdemona, certain hitherto undreamt-of facts concerning that Labyrinth down there under the Palace of Knossos. I was told these things when I had my little misfortune at the Roman Colosseum six months ago."

"Ya mean, when ya went missin' for all those weeks?"

"Arrrr."

"I thought I'd lost ya for ever. I'd no idea where you were!"

"Neither did I, at first. I was taken to a place that no one has visited and returned from, back to this earth, alive. It was a terrible place, Desdemona. A place where ghastly and mind-hurting things were happening everywhere I glanced."

"What were you doing – looking in a mirror all the time?"

Bone ignored her, and his voice crept lower, and became flat, as though all the emotion had drained completely from it. "I was shown things that people should never be shown. I was presented with scenes of history – great, infernal tableaus of humankind's failures and disasters and woeful, forgotten desperations!"

Desdemona became still ... she had never heard him talk like this before, with such dread in his tone.

He lowered his voice even more and this time, when he spoke, his words were slow and barely audible: *"I was witness to the machinations of the Underworld, Desdemona. Of the very void of nothingness, gloominess, hopelessness itself!"*

"Nevermore, nevermore, nevermore!" The raven shifted on the branch – even though she had only a small idea of what Bone was telling her, it was scaring her to her feather follicles.

"Luckily, after some time of wandering in this wasteland, I managed to escape from this place, through a fissure in the earth. There are many such fissures, my foul, feathered fiend, all around the world. One only has to know where to find them. But before I escaped,

 **56**

I learnt of this secret to do with the Labyrinth. I discovered that there did indeed exist something down there – *a special form of power* – that would enable me, Neptune Flannelbottom Bone, to achieve my rightful place as Dominator Majestic of the world."

Desdemona listened, her eyes throbbing. Even though she was being chomped to bits by the fleas, she dared not peck at a single one.

"There is a reason for everything, Desdemona. That was the reason I was thrust into the Underworld – to glean this information. Which, with my natural genius instincts, I did."

"Oh, brother." She could tell that he was returning to his normal, egomaniacal self and, in a strange way, she was relieved.

"And this is why we are searching that underground series of tunnels. This is why we are here. To find and harness this incredible power."

"What sort of power? Tell me, tell me, tell me!"

"Arrrr, not now. Not tonight. But I have a feeling that very, very soon, I shall be able to *show* you exactly what I speak of."

"You old windbag," she muttered under her breath. "Talk, talk, talk."

He shoved his cigar in his mouth and pulled out his gold fob-watch from his waistcoat pocket. "Hmmm. Nearly six-thirty." He put the fob-watch back and withdrew a handful of grubby coins. "Here, bird. Fly on down to that bakery again, the cheap one in the alleyway,

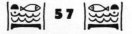

and get another two dozen of those bread rolls studded with sweet currants. And try and nick some cheese and olives while you're at it."

Partly because she knew he would not tell her any more of his great plan at this moment, and partly because her belly was growling with hunger, she agreed. "Aye, aye, my Captain."

"And don't dilly-dally. My stomach is sorely in need of sustenance!"

"It's sorely in need of its own postcode, if you ask me," she thought. She hop-fluttered down from the branch and into the cave. Emerging with a tatty, striped carry-bag in her beak, she hopped over to Bone.

"Make it snappy," he sneered, dropping the coins into the bag.

Without a squawk, she lifted her wings and flew off against the dimming night sky.

Bone watched her darkening shape disappearing into the distance. He remained there, on the boulder, finishing off his Belch of Brouhaha and studying the fading Palace of Knossos. Soon, he thought, as he blocked out the memories of his time in the Underworld, soon he would find the secret that lay beneath the ruined walls … the secret that would make him more powerful than he had ever been.

"Arrrrrrrrr," he sighed into the still night, his great hide bristling with unbridled anticipation.

LORE OF THE LABYRINTH

A STRONG, three-quarter moon had sailed out across the skies, majestic and magnificent, and beneath this glowing satellite, awash in its opalescent shine, soared Gerald Perry Esquire's small silver aeroplane.

Brenda sat, cross-legged, at the rear of the comfortable passenger cabin. The wide-awake Wonder Camel looked out through the round windows, watching the thin wisps of clouds filtering past and the scattered strings of stars hanging high above the wings of the plane.

Doris was perched on the armrest of Cairo Jim's seat. She had wasted no time in trying to find out more about the Labyrinth.

"So, what is it, why is it there, what does it do, who made it? Rark?"

Jim smiled and ran his forefinger over the feathers on the back of her neck. "My inquisitive dear, let me tell you."

Doris jerked up and down three times and got her claws comfortable on the armrest. Brenda turned her attention from outside and she, too, concentrated. (Even though she knew certain things about the Labyrinth from when she had accidentally eaten the

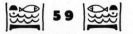

Encyclopaedia Britannica when she was a young and impressionable calf, she always relished Jim's telling of History.)

"It all goes back to ancient Greece," began the archaeologist-poet. "Back to the end of the Pre-palatial period of Crete, around about 1900 BC. Although much of the story of King Minos and his Labyrinth might stretch even farther back, possibly into the Neolithic period, to 3000 BC. Evidence has been lost in the mists of time."

"Neglected, near forgotten, obscured, 'In the dark backward and abysm of time'," quoted Doris from Shakespeare's *The Tempest*.

"Quaaooo," Brenda snorted, agreeing wholehumpedly.

"King Minos," continued Jim, "was the ruler of the island of Crete, and he controlled all the Aegean islands around it. He built a magnificent palace on Crete, at Knossos – when we arrive, you'll see the parts of it that were excavated and reconstructed in the years 1900 to 1906 by a bygone archaeologist named Arthur Evans. Evans was passionately devoted to the site, and he spent much of his life piecing together the life and times of Knossos … in fact, it was he who came up with the name 'Minoan' to describe this ancient civilisation. He named it, of course, after King Minos.

"Well, Minos was the son of Zeus, the king of the gods, so you can imagine he was a pretty important sort of king. Up in Athens he was feared, and often lampooned in the plays they put on there."

"Lampooned?" asked Doris, who wasn't familiar with the word – she thought it sounded like what happens when a whale is shot at with an indoor lighting appliance.

"Made fun of," explained Jim. "Mocked."

"Coo," cooed the macaw, blinking.

"But Minos was, as far as we know now, a wise and just king. Many of the greatest artists of ancient Greece – including the brilliant scientist, architect and inventor, Daedalus – came to live on Crete, and to create for King Minos.

"Minos had a wife named Pasiphaë—"

"Pasiphaë," Doris repeated, and Brenda snorted attentively.

"—and he also had, in his herds, the most beautiful bull in the world. It was a fine, magnificent-looking beast, and what Minos especially loved about it was its colour: it was pure, electrifyingly, *white*. From snout to hoofs, from tail to bushy eyebrows, there was not a hint of any other colour. It was as white as the first drop of snow on a sheet of white paper."

Jim stopped for a moment, his eyes gazing off into the far distance. "Hmmm. That gives me an idea for a poem. Aherm.

'It was only a bull from Knossos,
a bull of the purest white,
it meant not to harm or to boss us,
to scare us or give us a—'"

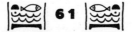

"Reeeeraaaaark!" screeched Doris, jerking her wings up and down. "Not now, Jim, get on with the story!"

"Quaaaooo!" came an encouraging snort.

"What? Oh, yes. That can wait I s'pose. Well, King Minos absolutely loved this bull … it was the finest, as I said, in all the lands. And this is where the trouble started. You see, Poseidon, the god of the oceans, had also noticed this magnificent white bull. He considered that it was far too good for King Minos to own, and thought that, because it was so fine and special, it should be offered as a sacrifice to a great god."

"Poseidon himself," Brenda thought gently.

"Poseidon himself!" squawked Doris. "Yes?"

"Yes," nodded Jim. "Poseidon told Minos that the white bull must be sacrificed to himself. But Minos refused. Minos believed that such a fine creature was far too good to be wasted like that. It was a very big mistake…

"Poseidon became furious when he discovered that Minos had disobeyed him. He swirled the oceans, sending colossal waves onto the shores of Crete. He summoned forth waterspouts that rose up out of the sea and dumped huge torrents of rain onto the island. He sloshed and slashed and slushed deep down there in the watery depths, and then, quite suddenly, he stopped. Poseidon had come up with a better idea to get revenge on Minos.

"Using his great powers, he cast a spell – light as the gossamer of a cobweb, yet stronger than girders of steel

– upon Queen Pasiphaë. It was a spell that was to herald the eventual downfall of Minos and the power of ancient Crete."

"Rark! What? Did he turn her into a toad? Did he shrink her down until she had to live in a matchbox? Did he give her a scrunch perm that she couldn't ever get rid of?"

"Oh, far worse than any of those, my dear. No, Poseidon cast a spell on Pasiphaë, so that she fell head over heels in love with the white bull of Minos."

"Well plait my feathers and call me Kylie!" Doris gasped.

Brenda shuddered – she always found this part of the story, and what was to follow, troublesome.

"Well," continued Jim, "unbeknown to King Minos, the queen went to the great inventor Daedalus and spoke of her love for the bull. She asked Daedalus to help her get closer to the bull, so that she could look into its eyes and whisper sweet nothings to it. So Daedalus made her a disguise, out of a cow's hide, and with a strong compartment inside it that the queen could hide in.

"Poseidon's spell grew stronger. Before long, the queen told the king that she was expecting a child. Minos was delighted – he didn't know that Pasiphaë was enraptured with his white bull, nor that Poseidon had put the spell on her. But when the queen gave birth to a son, and Minos saw the newborn baby, he was horrified! The baby, you see, had been born with the body of a boy, but with the head and horns of a bull!"

Doris was silent, her beak open and her eyes unblinking.

Brenda's breathing had slowed, and her humps were tingling.

"The baby – whom Minos called the Minotaur – grew very quickly. Both Pasiphaë and Minos turned their backs on him and, as he grew bigger, he grew fiercer. Minos realised he had to do something about the child. He summoned Daedalus and had him design and build an enormous, unfathomable underground maze, a maze hewn into the rock below the Palace of Knossos. A maze so confusing, so sprawling, so vast and dizzyfying, that no one – man, woman, beast or Minotaur – would ever have a chance of escaping from it!"

"This was the legendary Labyrinth!" thought Brenda.

"This was the legendary Labyrinth!" said Doris.

"It was indeed. At last, after a year and a month of building, the Labyrinth was completed. The Minotaur was chased into the dark, underground opening, fifty soldiers pursuing him with flaming torches and razor-sharp spears. He disappeared into the mouth of the Labyrinth, and the darkness swallowed him up like a gloomy thick blanket of punishment. His bellows – the agonised groans of the bull and the man – were heard echoing away into the subterranean prison."

"But..." began Doris.

"What, my dear?"

"He'd done nothing wrong, had he?"

"Nothing at all," thought Brenda. "Apart from being born."

"Nothing at all," said Jim. "Apart from being born."

"That's grossly unfair!" screeched the macaw.

"Unfair it was," agreed Jim. "And things only got worse for him. Minos must have felt some guilt for imprisoning the Minotaur in this way. Or maybe he used the Labyrinth and the imprisoned Minotaur to exercise his power. You see, he commanded that, every nine years, the Athenians must send seven young men and seven young women to be sacrificed to the wild and angry Minotaur."

"Rark!"

"Quaaoo!"

"Every nine years, the seven young men and seven young women travelled from Athens to Knossos. Every nine years, they entered the Labyrinth. Every nine years, not one of them returned.

"Then, Theseus, Prince of Athens, decided to pose as one of the seven young men. He travelled to Crete with the other thirteen people and went to Knossos, where he met King Minos. He also met Minos' daughter, the Princess Ariadne."

"Was she half bull too?" enquired Doris.

"No, Doris, she was all woman."

"Cooo."

"It seems Queen Pasiphaë had lost her affection for the white bull, or the spell had worn off or something.

Anyway, Theseus fell in love with Ariadne, and she with him. Just before he was about to enter the Labyrinth with the other young people, Ariadne gave him a piece of magical thread to wind around the rocks in the tunnels. This thread would help Theseus find his way out of the maze, after he had done what he was setting out to do...

"Thirteen young people entered the Labyrinth, their hearts filled with terror. The fourteenth, Theseus, was unafraid ... there was something in Ariadne's gift that set him firmly on his course.

"After three hours of wandering through the dark tunnels of the Labyrinth, with only the echoes of their footsteps and their own pathetic sobbings to greet their ears, they at last heard another sound: a dreadful, gnashing bellowing. It was surging through the rock walls, directly ahead.

"The bellowings grew louder, deeper, fiercer. It sounded as if the walls of the Labyrinth were made of the awful noise, as if the terrifying bellows were seeping into the rock, stretching it to a point where the whole Labyrinth might burst their eardrums!"

Doris's feathers were standing on end, and the hairs in Brenda's mane did likewise.

"Theseus drew his sword. He pushed the other young men and women back. Quietly he crept around the corner ahead..."

The aeroplane continued to drone through the night sky, but the noise of the propellers had dulled now.

It was as if, like Brenda and Doris, the aircraft was hanging on to every word of Jim's story and didn't want to miss anything.

"Theseus put out his flaming torch and turned the corner. There, in the gloom, five times the size of a robust soldier, crouched the Minotaur. His eyes shone in the darkness like two green lamps.

"Theseus knew that he must surprise the beast. The Minotaur, deranged and fierce from being locked away for so long, rushed at Theseus. Theseus sprang into the air. Just as the Minotaur reached the spot where Theseus had been standing, Theseus somersaulted in mid-air and fell onto the Minotaur's back. The creature was momentarily confused and, in that moment, Theseus lunged forward!

"The Minotaur tried to reach up, to drag Theseus from his back, but Theseus had been too quick – he had plunged his sword into the Minotaur's forehead. A great wailing filled the Labyrinth, louder and more fearsome than Poseidon's churning oceans. The powerful and wretched Minotaur flailed and crashed against the walls of his maze prison, but Theseus held on tight. As the creature rushed back and forth, screaming in agony, Theseus pulled out his blade and, with a swift slashing, he cut off the Minotaur's horns.

"There was a final, dazed, almost relieved burst of noise, and the Minotaur sank to the ground. The creature rolled over. And breathed no more."

In Brenda's left eye a single tear had formed. She

tried to contain it by closing her long eyelashes, but the tear escaped, rolling down her snout and dripping onto the carpet beneath her.

The plane continued to soar through the night, the noise of its engines rising again.

Doris was silent for a few minutes, her browfeathers wrinkling as she thought deeply. Then she squawked, "What's going on?"

Jim, too, had been thinking deeply. "Pardon, my dear?"

"With Bone," she said. "What's he looking for in the Labyrinth? I mean to screech, the Minotaur was killed thousands of years ago. And Theseus would've long gone, thanks to the thread of Ariadne. Yes?"

"Mm-hm," Jim answered. "He followed the thread out again all right, leading all the other young people to freedom."

"So what's Bone after down there?"

Brenda swished her tail and kept a thought deep in her humps. "Talos, perhaps?"

For once, her thought did not travel out from her. But something else came to Jim, and his skin erupted in a squadron of goosebumps. "I just remembered something."

"Rark! What?"

"Quaaoo quaaoo?"

"Something that our friend from the Greek Archaeological Museum wrote in a letter to me some time back."

"Euripides Doodah?*" asked Doris.

"Euripides Doodah," Jim confirmed. "He was writing to me at the time about the missing treasures of ancient Greece, and he happened to mention Crete, and the Palace of Knossos. He wrote – and I remember this as clearly as if I were reading his letter now – he wrote that many local people in Crete still believe that King Minos had imprisoned not only the Minotaur in the centre of the Labyrinth, but he had also hidden a vast, priceless horde of treasure down there."

"Coo," cooed Doris.

Brenda snorted with intrigue.

"His treasures didn't include only gold and silver and other worldly valuables. Oh, no. He also put down there untold marvels that had been invented for him by the brilliant Daedalus – things that no one else since then has possessed the knowledge to re-invent. Things that have been forgotten. Things containing great and startling power which haven't seen the light of day since ancient times!"

Doris slapped a wing across her eyes. "So that's why Bone's sniffing around!"

"When it comes to treasure and power, Bone will be lured like a pig to an overturned truck of rotting vegetables and food scraps." The goosebumps spread further along Jim's skin.

"What knowledge has he got this time?" Doris

See Cairo Jim and the Alabastron of Forgotten Gods – A Tale of Disposable Despicableness

conjectured. "For, knowing him the way we do, he wouldn't be going down there if he didn't have his mind set on something."

"That he wouldn't, my dear," said Jim. "Let's hope that when we arrive we can shed some light."

"In the meantime," thought Brenda, "let's have a look at these protective suits that Perry's supplied for us."

"In the meantime," Jim said, as the goosebumps began to subside, "let's have a look at these protective suits that Perry's supplied for us..."

◈ ◈ ◈ ◈ ◈ **6** ◈ ◈ ◈ ◈ ◈

INTO THE MAZE

"ZIP ME UP, BIRD, and this time watch where you put your beak. You almost caused me additional, unwelcome ventilation yesterday morning."

Desdemona regarded Bone through slitted, throbbing eyes. "Well, hold still, then," she croaked, as he hitched up his silver rubber suit and the stony, serious face of Joseph Lyons disappeared under the rubberware.

"I am perfectly still. Still and dignified."

"You're movin' around like you've got ants in yer pants." She picked up the zipper tag. "Nah, make that *antelopes*. There'd be room enough for a herd of 'em in *your* trousers."

"You insulting inkblot of ickiness. Zip me!"

The sun was beginning to rise over the eastern hills as Desdemona put the zipper tag into her beak and flew upwards. In ten seconds the overblown, self-proclaimed genius was zipped all the way to his neck.

"Arrrrrr." He puffed impatiently on his cigar.

Desdemona fluttered away from him, onto a slab near the East Bastion of the Palace of Knossos, where the opening to the Labyrinth lay under the concealment slab. She scratched at some fleas on the underside of her wing. Then she belched loudly.

"Uuuuuurpppp."

"Heavens to the Goddess Betsy," snarled Bone. "Have you no finesse?"

"Uuuuuuuuuurppppp," she belched again. "Must be them weevils I found in that bread roll I *finessed* this mornin'."

"Weevils?"

"Whaddya expect? I got the cheapest I could find at the bakery."

"I sincerely hope there were no such creatures in *my* bread rolls," Bone scowled. "My stomach is sensitive, as befits my high-powered brilliant disposition."

"I thought they were *currants* at first, but when I bit 'em I knew immoderately they were weevils. There was a big, fat one and a small one, both of 'em squirmin' about."

"And I suppose you ate *both* of them, you greedy glob of gruesomeness."

"Nope. Only ate the small one. I prefer the lesser of two weevils."

Bone scowled again at her, then nudged a large brown paper bag at her with his spat-covered ankle. "Here – take the prunes and drop them into the acid-filled drums. And make haste, Desdemona ... this morning looks like being breezeless, and I want the gas to spread before the first of the tourists emerge."

Grumbling, Desdemona took the paper bag in her beak. With a whoop-whoop-whoop of her dull black wings, she flew off to the acid-filled drums.

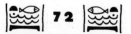

Bone clamped his cigar between his teeth. He had a final wriggle in his rubber suit, made sure his oxygen tanks were comfortable on his wide back, then bent over and pushed the concealment slab away from the hole.

By the time he had got it clear, the raven was back, her small rubber suit and the old, stained handkerchief under her wing, her eyes throbbing even harder than usual, from the initial rush of the vile prune-gas stench.

"Oh, brother," she moaned, "that stuff's more foul than one of your shirts after you've had it on for seven days straight!"

Bone ignored her and, instead, took a big sniff of the air. The hairs in his flared nostrils started to itch, and he knew the gas was doing its job. Quickly he took off his fez, secured his gas mask over his face, replaced the fez and shoved his cigar into his mouth through a hole he had made for that purpose in the gas mask.

Then he clambered awkwardly down into the hole.

"Hey, wait for me, you great flabby metropolis!" Desdemona plunged herself into her rubber suit, flapping and gyrating until the folds began to envelop her wingtips, tarsometarsus and other places of raven sensitivity.

"Get down here, you pathetic pastiche of poultry!"

She zipped herself up, being careful not to catch any feathers in the zipper (she had done this a few days ago – it was not pleasant, and it had affected the way she walked). Then she wrapped her stained handkerchief around her beak and hopped down into the hole.

 73

"Arrrr," mumbled Bone, swiping her away from his fez. He had already used his cigar to light one candle, and it glowed in the holder that was mounted at the front of the little wagon. "Light the rest of the candles, while I shut us in."

"Aye, aye," she croaked. As Bone manoeuvred the large slab back across the hole, she struck a match against the nearest surface.

"*Yaaaaaaaarrrrrr!*" howled Bone, as the nearest surface happened to be his bottom and, even through the rubber, he had felt the journey of the match head and the brief flash of heat against his person.

"Pardon me," said Desdemona.

"When we are finished down here, you shall be a very sorry and forlorn bird," growled the fleshy man through his gas mask.

He reached up to slide the slab back across the final few centimetres of the opening, and stepped down the rough steps. "I would use your head for a football if I did not want to conserve my energy," he told her, puffing a shaft of smoke into the heavy air.

"Yeah, yeah, yeah."

Now all the candles that were attached to the little wagon were lit, and the rock walls were glowing dimly but strongly enough for Bone and Desdemona to be able to see ahead for at least four metres.

"One last source of illumination," came Bone's muffled voice through his gas mask. He lit another candle, held it for a moment at an angle, and let the

hot wax dribble down onto the top of Desdemona's skullfeathers.

"Yeeerrraawwwwwllllgghhh!" she groaned, half in agony at the searing burning sensation, and half in relief because the wax had burnt a dozen ravenous fleas to death.

Bone righted the candle and pushed it firmly onto the top of Desdemona's head, where the hot blobs of wax glued it securely into place. "That's about the brightest thing that will ever come from your head," he muttered.

"Oh, why couldn't I have listened to my mother, and gone and settled down with some melancholic poet?" the raven lamented. "Why did I ever decide to hitch me wagon to you?"

"Speaking of which..." said Bone, grabbing the harness attached to the little wagon and fastening it around Desdemona's neck. "There. Your usefulness is once again realised."

"Ugh," she grunted, getting used to the weight.

"Now, come, let us not dilly-dally further. For today may very well be the day when I find my new and true power."

He turned away from her and strode boldly down the dimly lit passage. With a hop and a ground-laden flutter, Desdemona followed him.

On through the passage they crept, moving carefully down the gradually sloping floor. They knew this part of the tunnel well ... this was the place they entered and emerged from every morning and evening.

Soon, when they had descended deeper under the ground, and when the temperature had dropped considerably, they came to a spot where the passage ended in a wide wall filled with doorways. Bone had counted the doorways on the first day he and Desdemona had ventured down here, and he had been astonished at how many there were.

"Arrr," Bone arrred. "Here we are again. The entrance itself. Which of the eighty-seven untried doorways shall we take today?"

"Ugh. Search me."

He had previously made his mark – a small, blackened N which he had burnt onto the rock with the end of his cigar – next to the doorways he and Desdemona had already ventured into. Now he studied all the doorways where he had not made his mark, trying to decide which one they would explore today.

His eyes sleered across the dark holes, trying to detect some sort of clue – a variation in the light beyond, or a sign of wear on the rock floor leading into these dim places. But it was no good. They all looked the same: roughly hewn openings in this forgotten underground maze.

He puffed on his Belch of Brouhaha and frowned inside his gas mask. Then he began to chant:

"Eeny, meeny, miney, mo,
through a darkened hole I go –

Time comes with me, hour by hour
as I hunt my awesome power.

"Come, bird, down this one today. Keep your eyeballs open, and your hearing on its toes. Any small disturbance, apart from yourself, you must report to me at once."

"Aye aye, my eye," she rasped.

He took the cigar from his gas mask and made his small N on the rock next to the doorway. Then he ducked his large body through it, and disappeared into the gloom, like a huge, dull, silver slug being swallowed up by the earth.

Desdemona shook herself and followed, dragging the little wagon and wondering just how she was supposed to keep her hearing on its toes. Sometimes, she thought, her companion had far too much to say, and not enough words to say it with.

Brenda the Wonder Camel power-hoofed her way out of Iraklion Aerodrome and onto the road leading to the Knossos ruins.

The rising sun gilded the fine hairs in her mane and the luxuriant hairs in her impressive eyelashes as she pounded the roadway. She swallowed down the sweetish air, which was fresh with dew and other pure aromas, as her hoofs crashed onwards.

"Rark! Good pace, Bren! Keep it up!" Doris was perched on the saddle's front pommel. Her feathers

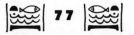

billowed in the airstream from Brenda's speed.

"I think we turn right at the next corner, my lovely," Jim called to his four-footed friend.

"Quaaaooo!" She came to the corner and turned smoothly to the right.

Onwards she galloped, through the quiet streets of Iraklion, past the closed shops and stores which, in an hour or two, would be opened and selling their wares: exquisite wax-seals and antique fabrics; fresh fruits and vegetables; hot loaves of bread and special Cretan wedding loaves, and gaudy plastic souvenirs of miniature Knossos Palaces and happy-looking rubber dolphins.

Soon Brenda had reached the outskirts of the city, and she picked up her pace. Gallop by gallop, the shops and houses started to fall behind, and within minutes, Brenda, Doris and Jim were surrounded by rolling green hills and big, spreading trees. The roadway became rougher, and Brenda's hoofs dug more firmly into the bitumen with every step.

A signpost loomed ahead.

"'PALACE OF KNOSSOS'," Jim read aloud. "'TWO KILOMETRES'."

"Quaaooo!" Brenda passed the sign, galloped up the hill, came to the rise and, with no warning, stopped dead.

"*Reeeeeeraaaaaaark!*" screeched Doris, somersaulting into the air from the sudden halt.

"*Whoooa,*" cried Jim, falling forward against the back of Brenda's neck, but still managing to remain in the saddle.

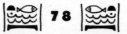

"QUAAAAAOOOOOO!" Brenda rolled her head and neck in wide circles.

Doris fluttered back down and landed on Jim's shoulder. "Something down there's upset her," she squawked.

Jim reached below, took out his Scatter Your Obscurity Archaeological Binoculars from one of Brenda's saddlebags, and raised them to his sun-spectacles.

His gaze scanned the scene: a small valley, wooded with forest and dotted here and there in the topmost reaches with a few houses. He moved his binoculars to the right and there he saw what he knew he would see: the red-painted columns and half-reconstructed stone walls of the Palace of Knossos and its surrounding buildings.

"It's Knossos," he told Doris.

"No," Brenda thought, her nostrils flaring. "It's something else…"

"No," said Doris, her wings twitching with concern. "It's something else that's spooked her. She wouldn't have stopped like that just because of Knossos."

"You're right, my dear." Jim reached forward and stroked the side of Brenda's neck. "What is it, my lovely? You've seen more ancient sites than any other Wonder Camel in existence. It's not those ruins that've spooked you. What's the matter?"

Brenda's extra-perceptive Wonder Camel sense of smell had detected the aroma of the foul and dangerous

prune-stench gas that was slowly seeping up from the bottom of the valley. It was travelling in their direction and spreading invisibly across everything below them.

Even at this distance, the supple hairs deep inside the back of Brenda's snout were quivering and beginning to itch.

"Quaaaaoooooo! The gas! The prune-gas is coming!"

Jim kept stroking her neck. "What's got into you, Brenda? What do you—?"

Then, with no warning, Brenda let out a huge and rarely heard Wonder Camel sneeze.

"AH–AH–AH–QUUUUUUAAAAAAAAAAA
OOOOOOOOOHOOOOOOOOOOOOOOOSHHHH
QQQQUUAAOO!"

"*Reeeeeeeerkkkk!*" screamed Doris as she was hurled into the air once again.

"*Whoooooooooaaaaaaaaa!*" yelled Jim as this time he was thrown clear out of the saddle. He landed on the grass at the side of the road with a soft thud.

Brenda shook her head violently – sneezing was a thing she did not enjoy. It would take minutes before her humps stopped tingling. "The gas," she thought earnestly. "The gas is coming!"

At last Doris received her warning. "The gas! Jim! She can smell the prune-gas stench already! It's coming!"

Jim scrabbled about in the grass, found his pith helmet and special desert sun-spectacles, and put them

back on. Then he leapt to his feet and ran to Brenda's saddlebags. "Okay, my friends," he said urgently, "let's get into these. And hurry!"

He pulled out all three of the special protective suits that Gerald Perry had provided. "First, you, Doris. Raise your wings, my dear."

"Rightio."

She raised her wings and her beak at the same time. Jim took the lightweight silver suit – it was barely heavier than a long cobweb – and pulled it down over her feathers, being careful not to catch her anywhere. He secured the Velcro straps just above her claws, and all the way up her front, finally encasing her head. From the circular opening at the front, her eyes and beak popped out.

"Snug fit since last I wore it, when we went under the Red Sea. I think I've gained a few pounds."

"And it suits you, my dear," said Jim. Gently, he popped the special goggles over Doris's eyes. Then he moved the small breathing-tube-air-filter across her beak and she sniggled it into place.

"Very clever of old Teddy Snorkel to make this so we can speak and breathe at the same time," Doris observed.

"Now, Brenda," said Jim. "You'll have to lend me a claw, Doris – this is a bit big for me to do on my own."

"Too right," said the macaw.

Jim removed Brenda's saddle. Together, he and Doris draped the huge, lightweight silver suit over Brenda.

Jim ensured that the humps and tail pieces were in the right position, while Doris flew under the Wonder Camel's belly and Velcroed her up.

Jim crouched and secured the fastenings around her hoofs. Doris pulled the hood over Brenda's head, making sure the goggles and the bits around her snout weren't too tight.

"Quaaaaooo," the Wonder Camel snorted gratefully as Jim slipped the breathing-tube-air-filter across her nostrils. Then he threw the saddle and saddlebags over her silver humps and strapped them securely around her.

"Now you, Jim!" Doris said bossily. "And be quick! We don't want you getting that rash all over yourself! Not that I'd mind rubbing lotion onto your skin, of course, I'm just thinking of the discomfort and the itchiness you'd have to go through, it'd be a real nuisance, especially when you're riding around on Bren's saddle all the time, ooh, rark! And the chafing you'd get ... well, that'd be positively undesirable, and the last thing we want is our Jim of Cairo all red and scaly like a—"

"All done," announced Jim, who had slid into his suit and fastened it while Doris was squawking on. He shoved his breathing-tube-air-filter under his nose, securing the tube around the back of his head.

"And not a moment too soon," thought Brenda. "The gas is thickening…"

The three of them watched, silently, as the prune-

stench gas swirled thicker and thicker. It closed in on them like a vaporous blanket.

"Don't breathe it in through your beak or snout," Jim instructed them. He mounted Brenda's saddle and held out his arm. Doris flew up and climbed his arm to perch on his shoulder.

"Let's go, my lovely," he said, gently nudging Brenda's sides with his Sahara boots. "Let's see what that deranged madman is really up to."

A TALOS TO ABUSE

DEEP UNDER the Palace of Knossos, Desdemona was itching and angry.

Her anger stemmed from what Bone was making her do, every five metres, with her razor-sharp beak on the cold, hard walls of rock that surrounded them. It was demeaning, she felt, not to mention painful.

The main source of her itchiness was, for once, not her infestation of fleas. Even though they were chomping and gnawing and nipping away at her prickled flesh close to her feathers, she had a more urgent itch right now: *curiosity*.

Bone had been speaking of this 'power' he was going to find in this Labyrinth. He had been mentioning it as if it was the greatest discovery he was ever going to make. He had gone on and on about it like he was an old-fashioned gramophone record whose needle was stuck in a groove and was playing the same old thing over and over and over.

The repetition was almost driving her sane.

She could take it no more, this being fed snippets of his plan, and not the whole thing.

She had had enough.

"SCRAAAAAAAAARK!" she scraaaaaaaaarked loudly

behind the large fleshy man.

He jumped, dropping his cigar to the floor. "You horrific hunk of hoo-ha! How dare you?"

"I want answers," she croaked, her eyes throbbing angrily.

"What on earth are you drivelling about?" He bent over and looked for his cigar.

"I wanna know what we're doin'," she said. "For the past month, we've been comin' down here, the same thing day after boring, trudging day! Looking for this thing you want so desperately. This thing that'll give you your precious 'power'. Sheesh! Well, I've had enough!"

Bone stopped searching, and straightened his huge body. "You've had what?" he hissed.

"Enough! I'm fed up with yer ambition and your secretiveness. I'm part of this team too, ya know! I'm here, doin' all the hard slog, ruinin' me beak, scrapin' it every five metres against these cold, hard, awful walls—"

"How else do you think we could find our way out if you didn't leave an arrow-shaped gash here and there to mark our way?" Bone asked, sneering at her.

"I've been loyal to you! I've followed your orders! I've been obliquient! And I tell ya this: unless you inform me exactly what we're looking for down here, right now, right this very momentum, I'm not takin' another clawstep! And ya can forget about me gashing into the walls! No, siree, I mean it. Ya can find yer own

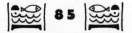

way outta this laburnumth. If ya don't let me in on it, I'm off!"

"You have been off since the day I first met you," Bone said, scowling. He wiped off the end of his cigar, put it to his gas mask, and took a big drag on it. He looked at Desdemona and thought about what she had said. Though he hated to admit it, she was right: for the moment, he *did* need her. Or, to be exact, her beak. Without it, he would surely get hopelessly lost and distressed in this unfathomable series of tunnels.

"Arrrrr."

"Arrrrr?" The candle wax dripped down Desdemona's head, narrowly missing her eye. "Whatsat supposed to mean?"

"It means that I have decided, in my generous way, to divulge some more of what my Great Plan of the Future is."

"Ya mean you're gonna tell me?"

"Enshut your beak and listen."

She unhitched her neck from the harness of the little wagon and plonked herself down on her belly, cupping her beak in her wingtips. "Go on, go on, go on," she croaked. "What're we after, then?"

Bone took a sniff of the air. "I think we are far enough under the ground, away from those noxious gases above, to remove these now." He pulled off his gas mask, tossed it into the little cart, and replaced his fez onto his greasy hair. "It's always struck me as strange how there is always fresh oxygen down here."

Desdemona took off her gas mask also. "The only noxiousness down here has a fez on its head," she thought.

Bone started peeling off his protective suit.

"Come on, come on," said Desdemona. "Tell me!"

"My plans of Brilliance and World Domination," he commenced, "have always, for one reason or another, come to a sorry end. All because of one thing. Do you know what that is, Desdemona?"

"That goody-gumbum Cairo Jim and his awful little gang?"

"No. No, no, no! It has been mere *coincidence* that he always manages to appear and get in my way. The day will come when I shall out-thwart him, and he will no longer be able to versify or to pursue what he stupidly thinks of as *goodness*." Bone shuddered at the very word. "No, I have been *lacking* one thing. If I had had this one thing at my side during the past ten years, I would never have suffered my setbacks."

"What is it? Humility? Good Manners? Cleanliness?"

"Enshut your beak, if you want me to answer your question. What I have lacked, is sheer brute strength!"

"Eh?"

"Physical power, Desdemona, huge, muscleman vigour! You are useless when it comes to this requirement. When it comes to strength, you are about as useful as a wart on an orange. And about as attractive."

Desdemona snapped her beak, but said nothing ... she was becoming curiouser and curiouser.

"Oh," he continued, "in the past I have tried to capture strength to aid me. That great hulking Herakles turned out to be no good at all, when his charm wore off."★

"The great stone brute!" blurted Desdemona.

"And the entire Turkish Women's Olympic Championship Tent Erection Team, which I so expertly *persuaded* to come to Sumatra with me, were not strong enough in the end."★★

"The great moanin' brutesses!"

"No, what I truly need is some huge source of strength that will obey me, without question, and overthrow my enemies willy-nilly."

"Since when are they our enemies?"

"Suppose I – what?"

"Willy and Nilly? I didn't know we were havin' arguments with *them*."

"Oh, how I wish someone would invent intelligence pills. I would buy the world's entire supply and pour them down your throat."

"Ergh. No thanks."

"Forget Willy and Nilly, and listen to me."

"Crark."

"Suppose I were to tell you that there existed

★ See *Cairo Jim and the Alabastron of Forgotten Gods – A Tale of Disposable Despicableness*
★★ See *Cairo Jim and the Lagoon of Tidal Magnificence – A Sumatran Tale of Splendour*

thousands of years ago, on this very island of Crete, a giant bronze robot who patrolled the coastline of the island. The robot was named Talos, and it was a marvel of engineering. King Minos – the man who built this Labyrinth and the Palace far above us – allowed Talos to roam freely, for the robot defended the island against all invaders and enemies."

Desdemona's beak began to open slowly.

Somewhere, far off in one of the dark tunnels, the sound of a drip of water falling onto the stone echoed plinkingly.

"This robotic giant, this 'brazen watchman', as the ancient tales describe it, was supposedly a gift from the great god Zeus to Minos. I heard all about Talos when I myself was entrapped for that brief amount of time, deep below the Colosseum in Rome.

"I also heard that Talos was animated by a divine liquid that circulated right through its colossal body. The robot was so strong, so monumentally huge, it could lean forward from the coast and pull out a dozen wide sailing ships from the ocean in the same way that I would pluck a bunch of grapes from the vine!"

Desdemona's eyes throbbed as she listened.

"And I heard, raven, when I was deep down under the Colosseum, I heard the most wonderful thing: that Talos is still in our sphere of existence."

"Eh?"

"The robot is still animated. It still operates. But not on the earth, oh no. *Under* the earth!

"It has always been believed that Minos lured Talos to this Labyrinth, where Minos knew his enemies would never find it. You see, the king planned to bring it out, when the enemies were besieging the palace ... somehow, on one of their raids on Crete, these enemies had got past Talos at the coast, and were advancing on Knossos.

"But then tragedy occurred... Minos and the Palace of Knossos were ransacked, and Minos did not have the chance to bring Talos forth to vanquish his enemies. Talos the bronze robotic giant was left, somewhere down here, to endure the anguish of eternity.

"Until now," Bone whispered. "Until I locate it. I shall lead Talos forth, and with it at my command, every nation shall bow to me! The oceans, the mountains and the lands far-flung shall all fall under the banner of Neptune F. Bone! And those petty government leaders small-minded enough to try to withstand my power – my colossal, unbeatable power – *shall be crushed beneath the very heel of Talos!*"

Desdemona took a huge gulp. Then she spoke in a quavering rasp: "And ya reckon that somewhere down here we'll find this Talos?"

"I am as sure of it as I am of my own Brilliance." Bone puffed maniacally on his cigar. "I feel, deep within my flesh, that today we shall enter halls of this Labyrinth that are deeper, taller and more ancient than anywhere we have yet been."

"Terrific," groaned the raven. "Just when I thought it couldn't get any chillier."

"Now, raven, peel off your suit. We must march forward."

"Why not? It's not like I've had any better offers." She got up and slithered out of her silver encasement.

"But before we go, come here!"

He lunged out and grabbed her by her throat-feathers.

"CWAAAARKKKKKK!"

"Time to make another little gash into the walls, Desdemona. We wouldn't want to lose our bearings now, would we?"

With a violent thrust he scraped her beak against the hard rock. In the fiery white sparks that shot out from the tips of her beak as it scratched deep into the wall, Desdemona beheld Bone's wild, crazy, illuminated eyes – eyes that had borne witness to the machinations and dark, dank secrets of the Underworld.

"AAAAAAARRRRRRRRRRRRRRRRRR!"

Part Two:

GREATER THAN ZEUS HIMSELF

8

KNOSSOS IN A FUG

THE GATES THAT SEALED THE ENTRANCE to the grounds of the Palace of Knossos were heavily chained and padlocked.

"Closed," Doris observed.

"No problem," Brenda thought.

"No problem," said Cairo Jim. He gave the Wonder Camel a gentle nudge, first with his right boot (encased in its silver protective suit), then with his left (similarly encased). Then he reached forward and trilled his fingertips against Brenda's rubber-covered mane.

Brenda knew the signal. Without a snort, she backed up two dozen paces from the gates, took a huge breath, bent her legs at the knees, and took a running jump.

Doris perched tightly onto Jim's shoulder, and he held on even more tightly to Brenda's reins as she soared through the air. Over the tops of the gates she went, as gracefully as a gazelle who might have had ambitions to be in the ballet.

With a heavy thumping of hoofs on the grassy verge, she landed on the other side.

"Beautifully cleared, my lovely," congratulated Jim, patting her on the neck.

 93

"The moon couldn't have sailed more smoothly," Doris chirped.

"Quaaaaaooooo."

"So here we are," Jim said, looking all around. "The Palace of Knossos."

Doris wiggled her beak behind her breathing-tube-air-filter. "This stench," she prerked, "is repulsive." Then she quoted from William Shakespeare's *The Tempest*:

"'The air breathes upon us here most

As if it had lungs, and rotten ones.'"

Jim and Brenda peered through the grey fog that seeped all around them. It moved slowly, in tendrilous wisps. It spread itself through the ancient half-walls and the columns ahead, like a serpent made of heavy, smelly air. It seemed to hang from the branches of the nearby trees, like matted weeds long smothered by decay.

Jim of Cairo shuddered.

"So," said Doris. "Millicent Spule told Perry that she saw the 'mysterious figure' get 'swallowed up by the ground'. So, where d'you reckon Bone's hole in the ground is?"

Jim pushed his pith helmet back and scratched the silver rubber on his forehead. "Good question. I guess I should've asked Perry if Millicent Spule had located it. Though if she had, I'm sure she would have told him, and he us. She's always been a very thorough person, has Millicent."

"A walk through the ruins is in order, then," Brenda thought.

 9 4

"A walk through the ruins is in order, then," squawked Doris.

Jim nudged Brenda's sides gently. "Come on, my lovely. Slowly into the Central Court. Let's all look out for any signs of disturbance near the ground."

With a flutter of her eyelashes, Brenda moved forward, along the pathway and up the steps that led into the Central Court.

"Whoa there," said Jim when she had reached the middle of the Court. She stopped, and he jumped swiftly down from her saddle.

Doris flew from his shoulder and onto a nearby slab of marble. She turned clockwise, beholding the excavated Palace of Knossos, with its columns and staircases extending all around the Court.

"Coo," she cooed at a row of three columns painted bright red. Even through the greyish fug, the red was vibrant and, it seemed to the macaw, pulsing with energy. "Jim?"

"Yes, my dear?"

"Were all the columns here red when Minos was king?"

"The outside ones probably were. And some of the interior ones as well. At least Arthur Evans believed so, when he was excavating here from 1900 for six years. He found traces of red paint on the ruined exterior columns, and when he reconstructed the interior columns he had them painted in the same red."

"Quaaaaooo," Brenda snorted. She imagined how

colourful the entire Palace and all its buildings would have been when everything was intact, and when Minos was powerful.

"He was a great archaeologist, was Evans." Jim walked slowly around the Central Court, examining every square centimetre of the ground for traces of Neptune Bone. "He unearthed not only the Palace here, but many other locations and artefacts as well. Another, smaller palace, a royal villa, a long Minoan roadway, ancient houses and tombs. And countless beautiful vases and urns and clay documents with hieroglyphics on them.

"Then there was the gold. Oh, I wish we'd been here with him. He found, in the west wing of the Palace, gold jewellery and objects made of crystal and ivory. Beautiful, exquisite things, including the Serpent Goddess figurine. She's made of gold and ivory, and she holds two writing snakes in her outstretched hands. Evans believed that she was the main Minoan goddess. He found her under one of the floors in the Palace."

"Coo," Doris cooed again.

Jim took off his special desert-sun spectacles and Doris and Brenda could see the excitement in his eyes. "Let's keep looking for evidence of Neptune Bone, but let's start again in a special place," he told them.

He turned and headed away to the western side of the Central Court. Doris fluttered after him, and Brenda lumbered, slightly awe-struck, after them.

Jim walked through a short corridor until he came to a room with a large, tall, stone chair set against one wall.

"The throne room," he told Doris and Brenda when they had caught up with him. "Evans discovered it in April 1900. That, we believe, is the throne of King Minos himself. As Evans told the King of Greece at the time, it is the oldest throne in Europe."

Brenda's humps tingled as they always did whenever she was standing at the places where History and Legend and Myth intertwined.

The back wall of the throne room was decorated with a fragment of a fresco showing a crouching griffin, the colours of which were still bright.

"It's a gorgeous painting," Doris said, lifting and lowering her wings in admiration.

"That it is, my dear. There're many gorgeous frescoes still left here, and others have been taken to museums in Iraklion and Athens. In fact, it was because there were so many artworks still surviving that Evans was able to reconstruct so much of the Palace. The paintings and pottery and frescoes and small clay models of houses he found were just like having ancient photos of the site to work from. It was a great resource."

"The past reconstructs the present," said Doris thoughtfully.

Jim smiled at her. "Come on, let's keep searching. I think we should go to the east wing ... there's something you both should see."

"I'm a very lucky macaw," Doris announced as she

flew after Jim, who was already making his way there. "I don't need to go very far to get to my east wing. Or my west wing, for that matter."

"Quaaaoooo," snorted Brenda.

Jim led them along the Palace's Stepped Porch, through the Sacred Repositories and the Pillar Crypts, down the semi-ruined Grand Staircase and back into the Central Court. All along the way, the three of them searched the ground and the tiles and the steps for any sign of Bone's disturbing presence.

The greyish stench continued to hang everywhere, filling up every nook and niche, curling around every dog-leg corner and passage, taking up the space like an unwanted visitor who doesn't know that it is time to leave.

"This way, my friends." Jim led Brenda, with Doris perched on top of her head, across the southern end of the Court.

They entered a wide, long hall, at the far end of which was a light well. A steady shaft of early morning sunlight fell through the shaft, onto the walls.

"This," said Jim, "is the Hall of the Double Axes. See down there, in the light well? There's a pair of double axes painted on the wall."

"Rark! I saw the same thing back near the staircase we came down!"

Jim nodded. "There are quite a few double axe paintings on the walls around here. You see, to the Minoans, the double axe was a sacred decoration.

 98

In fact, after Evans had deciphered some of the hieroglyphs from the stone tablets he'd discovered, he found that the Minoan word for 'double axe' was *labrys*."

"Labrys," Doris repeated.

"From which *Labyrinth* comes?" Brenda wondered.

"From which *Labyrinth* comes?" asked the macaw.

"From the very word itself," said Jim. "It's strange that these double axes are actually the only sort of weaponry Evans ever found here. There are no scenes of war or warfare or soldiers on any of the walls or floor mosaics, and he never found any swords or shields or spears, for that matter. He came to think that the whole Palace site was unfortified."

"Unprotected ... rark."

"According to one of the legends, Minos had a giant bronze statue who guarded Crete's coastline. Some scholars believe that because of this giant, King Minos didn't feel the need for an army or any soldiers to protect the Palace."

Brenda shivered, and the hairs on her humps pressed against her rubber suit as, one by one, they tried to stand on end. "Talos," she thought, but only to herself.

Doris scanned the floor of the Hall. "Doesn't look like there're any holes in there," she said.

"Come on then." Jim held out his arm and Doris flew from Brenda's head, onto Jim's elbow. She quickly hopped up onto his shoulder as he left the Hall of the Double Axes and approached another room.

Here, Jim stopped by the doorway, and Doris and Brenda both gasped at the exquisite fresco above the entrance.

"The dolphins of Knossos," Jim said, smiling, as he beheld the lively dolphins leaping across a vivid blue sea. Even though it was thousands of years old, the painting – apart from some small cracks – looked fresh enough to have been done last week.

They peered into the room, checking the floor. No holes or signs of disturbances lay there.

Jim took Doris and Brenda into another room, where there was another fresco. This one showed three men with an enormous bull. One of the men had just leapt right over the bull's head and horns, and had landed on its back.

"Some archaeologists have speculated that bull-leaping may have been an acrobatic sport in Minoan times, but we don't know for certain," Jim told Doris and Brenda.

The floor in this room was hole-less as well.

Doris thought about the men leaping over the bull as Jim took her and Brenda out of the Palace interior, and outside, to the East Bastion.

The air seemed to be getting thicker with the grey, prune-reeking fug. Doris flew from Jim and started waddling across the ground, trying to find any indication of an underground entrance.

Jim and Brenda spread out and they, too, looked carefully.

As far as ancient sites went, this was one of the neater ones that Jim, Doris and Brenda had been to. Often, pieces of ancient buildings had been left where they had fallen or where they had been damaged during plundering – but here at Knossos, slabs of marble and granite were for the most part neatly stacked in piles or leaning against the wall of the Palace.

Jim breathed in, slowly and carefully, through his breathing-tube-air-filter. The sooner we find Bone's entrance hole, he thought, the sooner we can get underground and hopefully evade this vile gas.

Brenda lumbered slowly along by a low wall, her snout close to the ground. She dragged her hoofs slightly, hoping that she might detect some sort of roughness in the ground that might have been caused by digging or other disturbance.

Doris waddled around, her rubber-encased wings clasped behind her back, her goggle-covered eyes beady and on the watch for a rough patch of ground.

Jim paced the Bastion, his brow furrowed beneath the silver rubber as he concentrated hard.

For ten minutes they continued searching. Then Jim went and sat on a marble slab that, unlike the others, was not part of a neat pile or stacked against a wall.

"Well, swoggle me up a tree," he said. "I don't know *where* that devious, conniving brute is disappearing."

Brenda came and stood by the edge of the slab. "It's got me humped as well," she thought with a frustrated snort.

"I'm as addled as a sozzled galah," Doris squawked, fluttering up onto the slab next to Jim.

"If only we had some more info to go on," Jim said. "If only one of the locals had told Millicent Spule exactly *where* Bone and that raven were entering the ground…"

A light blowing of air – cool and un-pruned – rose up from near Jim's right boot. It blew across the rubber suit, below the archaeologist-poet's right kneecap.

Still deep in thought, he gave his rubber-covered kneecap a quick scratch.

"Maybe," Doris suggested, "we should just lie in wait until tonight? If the three of us split up and wait at different points around the Palace, one of us might see Bone emerging."

"That's not a bad idea, my dear," said Jim. "But it means we'd have wasted an entire day. No, I think we need to keep searching for the entrance hole."

"Only a suggestion," said the macaw.

"And a very good one, too."

"Quaaooo," agreed Brenda.

Another minuscule gust of breezy air came up from near Jim's boot. Once again it blew across the rubber below his kneecap. Once again he absent-mindedly scratched his leg.

Brenda, out of the corner of her long-lashed eye, saw this.

Doris started pacing up and down the slab. "Perhaps he's erected a false column somewhere? One with a little door – no, make that a *big* door, knowing his size –

and he and the raven go into that and then down below? Maybe we should go round again, tapping all the columns to see if there's a hollow one?"

Jim considered the possibility. Another little breeze wafted up, and again he scratched at the rubber by his kneecap.

This time, Brenda had been waiting. She had watched, with her keen Wonder Camel eyes, the rubber in the area of Jim's leg right below his kneecap.

And she had observed that the rubber had rippled, gently like a cobweb, *upwards*.

Without a sound, while Jim and Doris were thinking, she lowered herself to the ground, her long legs folding under her. She moved her snout close to the ground where both of Jim's boots were resting.

Narrowing her gaze, she ran her eyes along the outsides of the soles of Jim's left boot. The ground there was smooth, except for a small darkened area of earth that was half under the heel of the boot.

The earth in this small, darkened area appeared to have been ruptured. Some of the dirt lay about in tiny clods.

Moving her neck forward, Brenda snouted at Jim's boot.

"What is it, my lovely?"

"Quaaaoooo." She nudged his boot, trying to get him to shift it.

"I think," Doris announced, "she wants you to move your boot away from the slab."

"Whatever," he said. He brought his leg forward, so that the back of his boot was no longer in contact with the front of the marble slab.

But this wasn't enough for Brenda: with a forceful shove of her snout, she spread both of his boots wide.

In a reflex action, Jim's left leg shot out to the left and his other leg to the right, and he rocked backwards onto the slab, like a beetle which has fallen back and can only roll upside down in its shell, helpless.

"Maybe she wants you to have a sleep, or something," said Doris. She had never seen Jim in such a position before. Certainly not in such a position designed by Brenda.

Brenda manoeuvred her jaw from side to side, so that the breathing-tube-air-filter came loose from one of her nostrils. She moved this nostril closer to the patch of darkened earth, which she could see – now that Jim's boot was out of the way – continued all the way up to the very edge of the slab.

She had a fair idea that it continued further, underneath the slab.

The extra-fine hairs in her nostril quivered across the ruptured earth. She stayed very still, and waited.

"I bet it's worms," said Doris.

"She doesn't have worms!" Jim said, sitting up straight again. "She's the healthiest Wonder Camel this side of Thebes."

"No, not that sort of worms," Doris squawked, jerking up and down. "Worms that she wants to *eat*.

I bet she's detected some worms under the ground there, and she wants to get at them and scoff them faster than you can say—"

"*Quaaaaaaooo!*"

Brenda's excited snort stopped Doris short.

"Took the word right out of my beak."

A cool, clear gust of air had come up through the ruptured earth, tickling the hairs in Brenda's nostril. She knew at once that there was a hole down there, and that the awful prune-stench had not entered it!

Rising to her hoofs, she took a step back. Jim squatted on top of the slab and watched her, as did Doris, next to him.

Brenda used her front hoofs to scrabble away at the earth that went up to the edge of the slab.

"I don't think it's worms," Jim said. "She's never dug that enthusiastically for worms before."

The dirt flew into the air, out between Brenda's rear legs, as she shovelled away. At last, after nearly a minute, she stepped back and gestured with her head and neck for Jim and Doris to look.

Together, they peered over the top edge of the slab.

"It's … a hole," Doris gasped.

Jim sprang off the slab. "You clever, observant, intuitive Wonder Camel," he enthused. "It was under this very slab!"

"Brilliant, Bren," cooed Doris.

"Quaaaaaooooo," she snorted.

Jim crouched down and squinted into the gap

Brenda had opened up beneath the edge of the slab. "Look! It goes under here." He stood and spat onto his rubber gloves. Then he leant over, placed his hands on the uppermost edge of the marble slab, and started to push.

Brenda lowered her head and put her snout hard to the slab, pushing also.

Jim grunted as he took the strain.

Brenda grunted too (not because it was a strain for her – she had a lot more mass to put behind her effort – but because she wanted Jim to feel that he was bearing the brunt).

Slowly, the big marble slab was slid across the ground and, bit by bit, the entrance to the ancient Labyrinth was revealed.

THE DESIGN OF DAEDALUS

CAIRO JIM PEERED into the hole. "It's wide enough, all right."

"Wide enough?" asked Doris, sticking her beak into the opening.

"For Bone to fit down. It doesn't extend very deep, but" – he squinted hard at the gloomy pit – "it looks like there's a set of steps that goes further."

Doris wasted no time. "Doesn't look too claustrophobic. Rark! Here we go, then!" She hopped down into the hole.

Jim and Brenda watched her silver-encased wings as she fluttered down the steps.

"Quaaaooo," Brenda snorted.

"You go next, my lovely," Jim told her. "If you suck in your humps, and go in on your rear legs first, you'll squeeze through the opening."

She fluttered her eyelashes at him, because that was a very good idea. Then she blew out all the air from her lungs, and snorted what was left out of her free nostril (the one that wasn't covered by her breathing-tube-air-filter).

Slowly, like a balloon being let down, her humps shrivelled until they sat almost flat against her back,

and her sides compacted inwards, so that her saddle and saddlebags appeared to be far too big for her.

She turned and backed up towards the hole. Carefully dangling her rear hoofs into the pit, she lowered her flanks. After a bit of scrabbling around, her hoofs found the top step.

"Take it slowly, Brenda," Jim said.

Tentatively she moved her hoofs onto the next step down, and then the next. By now, her front hoofs were at the rim of the hole. Brenda tucked those under her neck, and lowered them until they touched the top step.

With a fluttering of her eyelashes at Jim, she disappeared under the ground.

The archaeologist-poet straightened his pith helmet and adjusted his breathing-tube-air-filter. Then, taking it carefully, he stepped down into the hole.

The steps were rough – great chunks of rock that had been put there, it seemed, in a hurry. Jim watched his footing as he went down the first three steps.

Then he stopped.

"Rark!" On the floor below, Doris flapped her wings. "What's wrong, Jim?"

"Quaaaaooo?" Brenda turned and looked at him.

"I just realised something," he said. "The air down here seems to be fresh."

Doris raised her beak. "So it does," she prerked.

"Fresh underground air," mused Jim. "It must be coming from somewhere far away, where there's a gap or a fissure leading up to the earth's surface. Which

means I'd better fix this up now, before the pollution spreads down here."

He turned and climbed up the few steps. Reaching above, he gripped the edges of the slab that he and Brenda had pushed away. Then he grunted and heaved the slab heavily back across the hole.

"Good thinking, buddy-boy," said Doris. "Keep that vile gas of Bone's well out!"

Now that the slab was once again covering the entrance, it was almost pitch-black down here. Brenda took in a huge lungful of air, and her humps swelled and her sides filled out.

She lowered her head, stretched her neck around, and unfastened a strap on one of her saddlebags. Snouting in the saddlebag, she locked her jaws around a torch.

She pulled it out and, with her dexterous tongue, slid the switch on. A strong, white beam of light snapped out of the torch, lighting up the rough steps so that Jim could continue his descent.

"Good thinking, my lovely," he said.

As soon as Jim had negotiated the steps, Brenda flicked her neck and sent the torch sailing through the air. Jim reached out and caught it.

Brenda snouted in the saddlebag again, and took out Doris's torch (a smaller one than Jim's, with a handle that had been specially designed to be gripped by a macaw). The Wonder Camel lowered her head and Doris took the torch from her jaws.

"Thanks, Bren," she said, switching it on.

Brenda found her own torch and turned that on, too.

Together, the three of them lit up the surrounding walls and the floor ahead.

They were standing in a room, long and narrow and not much bigger than a train carriage, which had been roughly hewn out of the rocks. Here and there, parts of the walls glistened with water that trickled down in driblets from the ground above.

The floor sloped downwards, steadily but not steeply. At the lowest end of the room there was an opening in the rock wall.

Unlike the rest of the room, this opening had not been roughly made, but had neat edges and was mounted by a perfectly chiselled arch.

Doris fluttered up onto Brenda's fore hump. "That's the way, through there."

The three of them shone their torches across the opening. The darkness on the other side was deeper than where they were … it seemed like a wall of gloom, thick and dense.

Jim moved his torch beam up, and slowly around the archway. It had been fashioned from precisely cut rocks, placed intricately together.

His eyes caught sight of something chiselled neatly on the rocks. "Look!"

He grabbed Brenda's bridle and led her closer to the arched opening.

"Writing!" Doris screeched.

"Quaaaoooo!"

Jim's eyes widened as he beheld the finely formed characters. "That's strange," he murmured. "It's ancient Greek. I'd have thought that any writing down here would have been in the Minoan script."

"Lucky it's not," said Doris. "Minoan is not an ancient style of writing I'm familiar with. Matter of fact, it's one of the *only* ancient styles I'm not familiar with. Ancient Greek, on the other hand, is a piece of pie!"

"Decipher it, my dear. What does it say?"

The macaw raised her torch and moved the beam steadily across the writing. When she got to the end, she moved the beam back to the beginning and repeated the procedure.

"Oh, by my feathers, this is—"

"Doris, what does it say?"

"Take a deep breath," she told Jim and Brenda. "This is BIG." She cleared her throat, and read aloud:

"'HEREIN IS THE LABYRINTH. BUILT FOR MINOS THE KING, MINOS THE WISE, MINOS THE DECEIVED. LABOURED ON FOR A YEAR AND A DAY BY HIS GOOD SUBJECTS. DESIGNED BY THE HAND THAT INSCRIBES THESE STONES – DAEDALUS.'"

"Well swoggle me stratigraphically!" exclaimed Cairo Jim.

"Daedalus the inventor, himself," thought Brenda, swishing her rubber-enclosed tail against the cool air.

"Daedalus the inventor, himself," Doris cooed.

"That explains why the writing's in Ancient Greek, rather than Minoan," Jim said. "Daedalus was from Athens, originally, and not from Crete."

"Rark! Imagine! We've found the entrance to the Labyrinth!"

A chill crept through Jim's veins. "Unfortunately, my dear, we haven't."

"Eh?"

"No, we haven't found it, it's *Bone* who's discovered it. And we've got to discover *him*, and fast, and find out what he's up to."

"Right you are," said the macaw.

Brenda took a huge sniff. "The air coming from the other side of the arched doorway is even purer than where we are," she observed silently. "There is not even a trace of prune-gas stench."

Jim, too, had a big sniff. "You know something?"

"What?" Doris asked.

"Quaaaooo," snorted Brenda, who had something of an idea what he was going to say.

"The air. The air coming from through there is even purer than here. There's not even a trace of that dreadful prune-gas stench."

Jim began undoing the Velcro fastenings on his rubber suit. "So, we can get out of these things," he said, happily. "No danger of skin infection down here."

"Great," squawked Doris, putting down her torch and peeling off her suit as well. "It was like moving

around in a rubber glove. I've been wanting to stretch my wings and flutter my feathers something fierce!"

When she and Jim were out of the suits, Jim removed Brenda's saddle, and they both assisted Brenda out of her silver suit.

"Quaaaooo," she snorted gratefully, as Jim re-saddled her and secured her saddlebags. Doris bundled all three silver suits into Brenda's nearest saddlebag.

Jim smoothed down his extra-wide Sahara shorts, and tucked his gaberdine shirt in around the back, while Doris juddered her feathers all over. Brenda shook the hairs in her mane, and was glad to feel air wafting around her flanks, and not around the rubber protective suit.

When they had straightened and juddered and shaken themselves to their satisfaction, Doris said, "Well, through the arched doorway it is. Let's go. Rark!"

She led the way, waddling down the rest of the sloped floor and stopping in the centre of the doorway. Jim followed her and stopped next to her. Brenda came and halted behind them.

They shone their lights into the dark void. The beams from the torches lit up the other side, but only feebly.

"Look," whispered Jim. "It gets wider."

"And the floor keeps sloping downwards," observed Doris.

"Quaaaooo," snorted Brenda.

"And it's cooler. Much cooler," Jim said.

A far-off *plink*ing sound broke the silence.

"Somewhere through there is water," Jim whispered. "I'll bet my pith helmet it's fresh. We'll be able to refill our water bottles if we find it."

"Let's go, then," said Doris, gripping her torch firmly in her wing and waddling under the arch and down the sloping floor.

Cairo Jim followed her, keeping one eye on the floor ahead, and one eye on his macaw friend.

Slowly, Brenda passed under the arch of Daedalus. As she followed her friends down the floor, she thought she heard – for the briefest of moments – a low, deep sound coming from somewhere far ahead.

Only Brenda heard this sound, thanks to her highly sensitive Wonder Camel hearing.

It sounded to her like a moaning ... a moaning full of hopelessness, and heartfelt enough to pass through the tonnes of rock around them.

The Wonder Camel raised her head and pricked up her ears, to try and hear more of this deep, sad sound. Was it the wind, blowing through a cavern, far away? Was it the slow movement of the under-earth, the rocks stretching infinitesimally, making a noise that only could be audible so far beneath the ground?

Brenda did not know, for as she tried to hear more of this seeping moaning, it stopped as abruptly as it had started.

◇ ◇ ◇ ◇ ◇ **10** ◇ ◇ ◇ ◇ ◇

HOURS OF TORCHLIGHT

"SCRARK! Can we have a break? Puh-lease? We've been skulkin' for hours!"

Desdemona's eyeballs throbbed wearily as she hauled the little wagon along yet another dark, dank passageway.

"Not yet, my crude cartel of cruddiness." Bone pulled out his gold fob-watch and flicked open the cover. "It is only three hours since we entered the Labyrinth. We have many more hours to search before we can permit ourselves the luxury of – as you put it – a break."

"Ratso," muttered the raven.

Bone put his fob-watch back into his waistcoat pocket and moved further down the passageway. After a few steps he stopped and declared, "Make your mark, bird!"

"Here we go again," Desdemona croaked. She hopped over to the left-hand wall (the little wagon bounced along behind her) and grazed the tip of her beak sharply against the rock.

A fingernails-down-the-blackboard screech filled the passageway, and a thousand tiny sparks shot out from the wall.

 115

Desdemona rubbed her beaktips with a wing.

"Ooooh. I'm not gonna have any chompers left by the time we're finished down here." She spat a few lumps of rock out of her beak, and the fleas on the underside of her belly went on a biting spree.

"Enough of your lame protestations," sneered Bone. He held a candle at arm's length, and peered beyond it. As if a shadow had washed over him, his face filled with a look of mild astonishment, and the hairs in his beard bristled.

"Oh, this is hopeless," Desdemona rasped.

"I beg your pardon?" Bone contained his look of mild astonishment and turned his head in her direction.

"Well, I've been thinkin', and I've come to the concussion that this is hopeless."

"And they said that the days of miracles were past," Bone said. "Imagine it, Desdemona the raven tries out a new concept: *thinking*. Arrrrrr."

"Can it, chubbychops!"

Bone swivelled around on his heel and glared at her. *"What did you say?"*

"Listen, I've had a thunk about what you said earlier. All that stuff about this Talons statue."

"*Talos*, you cretinous clump of crudity."

"Yeah, yeah, yeah, Talos. Anyway, I reckon you've got as much chance of findin' him down here as you have of winning the Mr Slenderboy World Slimming Championships."

Bone raised a bristly eyebrow at her.

"Zilch," she went on. "Zero. Never in a million years. The same chance as a snowball in—"

"Arrr, you've made your point. And why, oh bird of brilliance, do you think that we won't find Talos?"

Desdemona rolled her throbbing eyes up to the ceiling (after making sure that no candle wax was dribbling down from the candle on the top of her head). "Just take a look at where we are," she uttered with disgust.

Bone looked up, then around at the walls. "Yes?" he sneered. "We are in the … let me see … ninety-fourth passageway that we have entered so far in this vast underground maze. So what?"

"Well," she croaked, "look how cramped it is."

His eyes narrowed, and a strange smile curled his fleshy lips. "Cramped?"

"Yeah. Up above. It's not that high, is it? I mean ta croak, it's big enough for *you* ta stand up straight in, but that's not sayin' much. You're not exactly a Harlem Globtrotterer, are ya?"

"There's no need to be snide. My mother always used to say that brilliance comes in small packages."

"If it came in *fat* packages, you'd be the most brilliant man in the world."

Bone took a step towards her, his fist raised, but she continued quickly.

"I mean, look at this place. Ya told me before that this huge statue was so big it could lean out from

the shore and pick up a boat in the ocean, right? Well, how on earth ... nah, make that how *under* the earth ... do you expect such a tall thing to fit in here?"

Bone's smile curled his lip even further, splaying the hairs in his moustache and flaring his bulbous nostrils. "I shall not administer punishment on you, Desdemona, for two reasons. Firstly, I need you to pull the little wagon – I am far too important, brain-wise, for such manual labour. Secondly, I would not want you to die in ignorance."

"Eh? Whaddya mean, *ignorance*?"

"I am going to show you the answer to your query."

Her eyes throbbed silently, as she waited for him to continue.

"You are, for once in your pathetic little life, quite on the ball with the observations you have made about the size of this passage. There is absolutely no way that an enormous statue like Talos could fit in here. But behold, raven ... behold the next stage of the Labyrinth!"

He turned away from her, holding his candle at arm's length again, and walked to the end of the passageway.

Desdemona took a big gulp, swatted at some fleas, and followed.

When she saw what he had already seen, her beak dropped open and her rough, yellow tongue drooled. "Well, fondue my tarsometatarsus," she gasped.

"Arrrr," Bone arrrred, his eyes shining in the candlelight.

There, before them, the passageway had opened into a colossal chamber that must have been as wide as three football fields side by side.

"It's hugeous," Desdemona rasped.

"But look up, bird, look up!"

Slowly, Bone raised his candle. Just as slowly, Desdemona's eyes followed the flame.

As the candlelight moved higher, Desdemona could see that the height of this chamber kept on rising. Up and up and up, until the feeble glow from the candle could not light up any more.

"I'll be sushied," muttered the raven. She stared up at the darkened reaches. "It seems to go on forever!"

"Arrrr."

"I'd no idea we'd come down so deep."

"You've no idea, full stop."

"How rude."

"Now *there's* height for you," whispered Bone. "Look, as high as a ten-storey building, or I'll eat my fez. And down there" – he waved his candle down the sloping floor, towards the far end of the chamber – "is another doorway."

"Crark." Through the dimly lit gloom at the far end, Desdemona could just make out the shape of an opening in the rock wall.

"From my studies of underground passage networks of the ancient Greeks when I was at Archaeology School,

 119

I am sure that from here on in, the Labyrinth will only get bigger and deeper and … more valuable to me. Arrrrr!"

He did a small jig on the spot, and all the faces of the Prime Ministers of Australia wobbled around in a bizarre and severe fashion.

Desdemona cringed at the wobbling faces, then she peered down the chamber. The walls at both sides rose up unevenly; at first they appeared to be straight, but then, a few metres up from the floor, they became rougher, and the angle of them changed, and then changed again. It was as if some drunken stonemason had chiselled them in a hurry.

"Them walls," she said. "They look like they can't make up their minds which way to go as they get higher. This way and that way, in and out. Sheesh, I've never seen such archetypeture."

"Never mind about the walls, it's that doorway that craves *my* attention. Come, and don't dilly-dally. Power lies before me, and I hate to keep it waiting!"

He strode off briskly down the slope.

Desdemona watched his capacious, face-covered bottom advance away from her. She had a quick shudder, then skittered after him, the little wagon bumping along behind her.

"Look," whispered Jim. "This must be the second true entrance."

He, Doris and Brenda had stopped before the wide

wall filled with doorways. Each of the doorways was tall and rectangular in shape, and the top of each had been carved to finish in a point.

Apart from the pointed tops, there was no other decoration of any sort.

"There're so many," cooed Doris, running her torchbeam across the wall.

"Let's count them," Jim said.

"Quaaaooo," snorted Brenda.

Silently, the three began counting the doorways. Jim started pacing from the centre to the right; Doris hop-fluttered across the floor from the left-hand wall, and Brenda stood well back so she could get a complete view of all of the doorways without moving.

It got a bit confusing after a minute or two, as their individual torchbeams darted this way and that, bisecting each other and causing Jim to lose count of which was the last doorway he had counted.

"Oh, blow it," he said, going over to the right wall and pacing to the left as he started again.

"One hundred and three, one hundred and four, one hundred and five..." counted Doris, being careful not to bump into Jim's leg as he passed.

Brenda counted silently, moving her torch across the centre of each doorway and marking the addition with a swish of her tail through the coolness around her.

Doris arrived at the right-hand wall. She turned and waited for Jim to reach the opposite one.

Brenda finished counting and waited, too.

"One hundred and seventy-nine," Jim finally announced, turning to his friends.

Doris blinked. "I got a hundred and eighty," she said.

Brenda thought, "The same as I."

Her thought pervaded Jim's mind. "A hundred and eighty," he nodded. He pulled out his notebook and quickly wrote down the figure, and made a rough sketch of the shape of one of the doorways.

Then Brenda gave a snort. "Quaaooo!"

Doris turned to her. "What, Bren?"

Jim looked up from his notebook.

Brenda came down the sloping floor and brought her torchbeam up to a marking on the wall, next to one of the doorways, at about the height of Jim's chest.

"Look!" squawked Doris. "She's found a … a sign or something."

Jim put his notebook back in his pocket and came over to them. "So there is," he said, examining the small, black **N**.

Doris flew up onto Jim's shoulder. She leant down, put her beak close to the wall, and took a sniff. "Rark! There's the very faint odour of smoke. I think it's been burnt into the rock."

"Hmmm," hmmmed Cairo Jim.

"And I'd say, fairly recently, too," the macaw observed.

Brenda flashed her light across some of the other entrances. "Look," she thought. "Quite a few of the other doorways have the same mark!"

Jim ran his light across the wall. "Look," he said. "Quite a few of the other doorways have the same mark, too."

"The sign of Bone," said Doris.

"Quaaaooo," Brenda agreed.

Jim frowned. "The vandal's been making his mark. With one of his stinking cigars, I bet. He's been ticking off each entrance he's gone into."

"Brute," Doris screeched.

"The question now," pondered Jim, "is which entrance do *we* take?"

Brenda flicked her head back and sent out a thought: "Which is the most recent mark Bone's made?"

"Rark! Let's find the most recent mark Bone's made, if we can." Doris jumped off Jim's shoulder and began flying close to the wall, past all the doorways that had the **N** mark next to them.

She flew slowly, bringing her beak close to each **N**, and keeping her eyes wide and alert. Occasionally she made a little announcement, such as, "No smell on this one," or, "This one's old, I think," or, "He must've been in a hurry when he made this one … the burn mark is very light against the rock."

Jim and Brenda watched and waited, and helped out by shining their torchlights wherever Doris went.

Eventually, after more than five minutes of close inspection, she hovered in the air after sniffing one of the marks. "This is it," she announced. "The reek of

tobacco is stronger than on any of the other **N**s. If I'm not mistaken, it was made earlier today."

Jim went over to the wall and had a sniff of the **N**. He reeled back, his nose wrinkling. "Yergh. I think you're right, my dear."

"Want a sniff?" Doris asked Brenda as she flew onto the Wonder Camel's saddle.

With a polite snort and a shake of her head and mane, Brenda declined the offer.

"So," Jim said, "this is the one we go into. But first..."

He unbuckled one of Brenda's saddlebags and hunted about inside it, shining his torch within. Doris leaned over and stuck her beak in, which didn't really help Jim at all.

"Here it is," he said after a few moments of trying to see with Doris in the way. He pulled out his knapsack, which he had filled with his usual archaeological necessities: matches, a box of slow-burning candles, compass, special Old Relics Society penknife with thirty-seven implements, a small photograph of Jocelyn Osgood in a leather frame (the photograph was in the leather frame, not Jocelyn Osgood), a bunch of pencils secured together with an elastic band, and his newest writing book, just in case a poem came to him all the way down here under the earth.

"Right," he said, pulling the knapsack's straps over his shoulders. "Let's go, shall we?"

"Wait," thought Brenda. "There's just one thing."

"There's just one thing," Doris squawked, picking up

the thought and taking it further. "We'll need to mark our route, so we can find our way back again."

Jim smiled. "Good thinking, Doris. I don't know where I'd be without you and Brenda, sometimes."

Doris blushed faintly beneath her feathers. "So what should we use?"

Jim thought, frowning at the floor. "The ground's been too hard so far to mark. So we can't get Brenda to scrape her hoof on it, or anything like that."

Brenda snorted… Jim was right; if she scraped her hoofs repeatedly against the hard rock, it would be no time before the hardened outer casing of her hoofs began to split.

"And the same with the walls," Doris said, blinking.

"For once, a good bit of string won't do the job, either." Jim shook his head. "We've got a ball of string in one of Brenda's saddlebags, but it wouldn't be long enough. And besides, there's been nowhere so far to tie any string onto, or to wind it around. The passageway to here has been bare."

"Hmmm," Doris hmmmed.

"So there's nothing for it," said Jim. "Much as I don't want to deface the walls down here, I'm afraid I'll have to use my WINKLIE."

"Rark!" Doris jumped on Brenda's saddle. "Your *what*?"

"Quaaaooo," Brenda snorted with some uncertainty.

"My WINKLIE. I'll just daub it on the walls every few metres or so, as we go. That should do the trick."

Jim started rummaging in one of the saddlebags.

Doris looked at Brenda, and she turned her head and returned the look.

"Here we go," Jim said, pulling out an implement that looked like a cross between an overgrown pen and a paint gun. "My Waterproof Indelible Non Knobbly Luminous Ink Excretor."

"Oh," Doris squawked. "Your WINKLIE."

"The very thing. It's the latest bit of archaeological equipment to be approved by the Old Relics Society. It contains a glow-in-the-dark ink that will last for up to three weeks. Then it fades away, leaving the surface you've painted completely unblemished."

"Coo."

"Quaaaooo."

Jim held up the WINKLIE. "I've been waiting for the right opportunity to use it, and this is it."

Doris jiggled herself up and down, and flexed her yellow and blue wings. Her torchbeam swung in a big arc across the wall of openings. "Let's go, then. Time is winding its way onwards, and we don't want to waste it."

"You're right, my dear." Jim took hold of Brenda's bridle. "Ready, my lovely?"

Brenda rolled her torch to the other side of her jaws and nodded her beautiful head.

Jim pressed the WINKLIE against the wall. Then, together, their torchbeams lighting the way, the trio passed silently through the opening, and down the gloomy passage ahead.

TURNING A CORNER IN TIME

FOR NEARLY FOUR HOURS, Jim, Doris and Brenda ventured through the dark, cool, quiet passages of the Labyrinth.

They came to many corners – some which they could see before they reached them, far off at the end of a corridor; others that would appear suddenly, lit up without warning in the beams from the torches.

Every five metres or so, Cairo Jim daubed the WINKLIE against the rock wall. It left a soft, greenish splotch on the dark rock, which, after Jim, Doris and Brenda had moved on, glowed for several minutes before fading away to melt into the dimness around it. These splotches would glow again, the next time light fell upon them.

As the trio progressed through the great network of corridors and tunnels, the floor continued to descend. Sometimes it was a gradual downwards sloping, every centimetre taking them deeper and deeper underground. At other places, in some of the less wide passages, the floor would sweep down more sharply, to become almost a raked ramp that the three explorers had to negotiate very carefully, especially Brenda, who had to place her hoofs with care on the steep surface.

All through these deep, dark places, the silence swelled, broken only occasionally when Jim or Doris spoke, or when Brenda snorted quietly; or, every now and then, by a drip-drip-dripping of water, echoing like a gunshot, from somewhere far ahead in the unseen dimness.

Soon, other sounds could be heard: rumblings – soft but definite, growing louder with every passageway. Jim had them in his stomach, as did Doris. Brenda had them in hers, as well as in her humps.

"I think," said Jim, when the three of them were feeling their hunger more strongly, and when their rumblings had grown much louder, "that we should stop down there, at the end of this corridor, and have a spot of lunch."

"Agreed," Doris squawked, patting her stomach-feathers. "I feel like I've got baby thunderclouds rolling around in here."

Brenda fluttered her eyelashes – she knew the sensation well. She followed Jim and Doris to the end of the corridor, where Jim dumped his knapsack on the floor and sat heavily, leaning against the wall. "My legs are telling me to take these sloping floors more gently, I think." He rubbed his calf muscles, and stretched out his legs in front of him.

Brenda lowered herself against the opposite wall, and Doris waddled over to her and began poking her beak and a claw into one of the saddlebags.

"Here we are," she announced, bringing out, one after the other, a tin of imported Malawian snails, a packet of

freeze-dried worms and a can of Poshoglian's Braised Beef and Beetroot with Sautéed Chestnuts (a choice of Gerald Perry Esquire's). "Food at last!"

Jim arranged the torches so that there was enough light spread evenly about. Then he set about opening the cans with the tin-opener attached to his archaeological penknife.

A small stream of clear water was dribbling down the wall, and Doris opened her beak and darted her tongue into the dribble. "Pure," she said, blinking.

"I thought so," Jim said. "All this rock, so far down here, has purified it better than any human-made invention could hope to."

Doris held the opened packet of freeze-dried worms under the water. In little more than ten seconds, the shrivelled contents of the packet had swelled and fattened. Brenda snorted excitedly as the smell of mock-worms drifted out of the packet and up into her nostrils.

Then, as a far-off dripping *plink*ed away, Brenda slurped up her worms, Doris sucked up her snails and Jim forked up his braised beef and beetroot with sautéed chestnuts, each of them chewing silently and thinking about what might lie ahead.

The heavy footsteps of Neptune Bone slapped hard against the cold limestone floor and the vast, rock-hewn halls.

The first enormously high chamber they had passed through had led to a loftier chamber, and that into an

even more tremendous one. These had continued, each of them outdoing the one before it as its floor dipped further underground and its walls grew longer and wider and taller.

Now the chambers were so big they were almost incomprehensible to Desdemona. As she hopped after Bone, down the ever-deepening floors, with the little wagon behind her, she grew increasingly aware of the immense spaces that were all around. Even though her feeble candlelight did not carry far into the darkness, she could almost taste the dizzying height above.

"Boy," she croaked, "I bet it'd take me twenny minutes just to fly to the top of this dump. Sheesh! I've never known such huge places."

Bone was smoking a Belch of Brouhaha as he walked along. "Arrrr," he uttered, slowing his pace and looking all around. "I have. The Underworld, Desdemona, is a tangled, buried, towering place, much like this." His eyes narrowed and he blew a shaft of smoke upwards, through his moustache and bushy eyebrows. "Although it is more populated than here…"

"Boy, the sooner we find this animated junk pile and get outta here, the better. These walls are gettin' darker, ya know."

"Darker?"

"Yep. Look at 'em. They're almost as black as me feathers now. The deeper we go inta these cavernous holes, the darker the walls and the floors get."

Bone had been so busy keeping his eyes open for any sign of Talos that he had not observed the changing rock. He crept closer to one of the walls and held his candle to it.

A yellow glimmer reflected back off the rock, and in the sheen, he saw the dull white reflection of his own eyes.

"Arrr, you are right, you nasty noticer of the night. And look how the walls have taken on a reflective quality. They are becoming positively mirror-like."

"Well don't stare too closely," she rasped. "We don't wanna crack the place to pieces."

Bone turned and sneered at her. "Sticks and stones may break my bones," he retorted, "but drivel such as that urges me on in my quest with even bolder determination."

The raven shut one eye and squinted upwards. "They might be smoother on the surface, but they still look like they can't make up their minds which way ta go as they get higher. In and out. Snaking that way, then this way. Crazy, if ya ask me!"

"I hardly think that you are one to be levelling that accusation," said Bone. "I am of the firm conviction that when sanity was being handed out, you were hiding behind a door or something."

A flea bit Desdemona on her belly, and she wriggled around, trying to shake it off.

"When you are finished with your little dance, make another beak mark into the walls."

"Do I have to? The rock's harder, and my poor old choppers feel like they're celery stalks. They're gonna fray all the way up to—"

"Enshut your beak and gouge that wall!" Bone's eyes were wide with menace.

"All right, all right, all right." With a sigh, Desdemona dragged the little wagon over to the wall and pressed the tip of her beak into the wall's hard, glassy surface.

Just as she was about to apply pressure and scratch her beak across the rock, she pulled her head away and cocked it to one side.

"Did ya hear somethin'?" she asked, her eyes throbbing curiously.

"What?" Bone's beard bristled.

"Did ya hear somethin'?"

"Not a sound, you mutant moronic mess. What are you croaking on about?"

"I heard a sound," she said quietly.

Bone leant down towards her, his caterpillar-like eyebrows creasing. "A sound?"

"Shh!"

He waited for a moment, as Desdemona cocked her head to the other side, and then back again. Then she shook it slowly.

"What sort of sound, Desdemona? A bronze-like sound? The clanking of metal joints moving through a cavern ahead?"

"Nah. Nothin' like that."

"Well? What was it?"

She shook her head again. "It's gone now."

Bone grabbed her by her throatfeathers. "Tell me! What did you hear?"

"*Awwwwulllllgggghhhhhkkkk!* Leggo, you're squeezin' me lifeless! *Awwwwulllgggghh*—"

Bone relaxed his grip. "What was it that you heard?" he hissed.

"I thought," she gasped, her chest heaving and all her fleas doing cartwheels across her body, "I thought I heard a … a sorta *moanin'*. Deep, deeper than anythin' I've heard for ages. Like it was comin' from a long, long way off, somewhere…"

"And you can't hear it now?"

She shook her beak. "Nah, it's died away. Coulda just been the wind or somethin', blowing through all these passageways and hallways. Wind does funny things sometimes."

"Arrrr, you should know. You are the living breathing expert on what wind can do. Sometimes it is as though you have a cyclone trapped inside your belly."

"Crark. Trumpet-buttocks," she muttered.

"Now, are you going to gouge that wall of your own accord, or am I going to have to *persuade* you, yet again?"

"Nevermore, nevermore, nevermore!"

She turned her beak to the wall and wrenched the tip across it. The sound of splintering rock screamed through the dank air, and glassy sparks shot all around.

"Now come," Bone commanded. "And keep your notions of wind and all such thoughts to yourself."

He turned on his chubby heel and ventured off around another wide corner.

Desdemona rubbed her sore beak and, just for an instant, cocked her head to the side again. She was sure of it, she *had* heard something. And she had a good idea that it had been more than just wind...

◇ ◇ ◇ ◇ ◇ **12** ◇ ◇ ◇ ◇ ◇

AXE ME THAT AGAIN

"WELL, SWOGGLE ME ceremonially!" exclaimed Cairo Jim.

"Filibuster my feathers," Doris gasped.

"Douse me with dignity," thought Brenda the Wonder Camel.

The three of them had stopped, as one, when they had turned what must have been the two-hundredth corner since they had eaten lunch. There, suspended at the sides of the long, wide gallery in front of them, were two gigantic double-headed axes hanging with their heads downwards.

Both axes stretched from the high ceiling almost all the way to the floor.

Each axe had a blade on both sides of the helve*, and each axe had one of these blades facing in towards the centre of the gallery, with the other pointing out towards the wall behind it.

"They look like solid gold," Jim whispered.

"Amazing," Doris cooed. "They 'surprise me to the very brink'," she quoted from *Timon of Athens*.

"They're enormous," breathed Jim, running his

---

* Handle

torchlight all the way up the handles, to where they were attached by a pair of heavy chains to rings on the ceiling. "Those great spiralled helves. Those huge curved blades…"

"They also look sharp," Brenda thought. A huge involuntary shudder passed through her humps, and the hairs at the very end of her tail stood on end.

"They also look sharp," Doris observed, shining her torchlight over the blades that were positioned inwards. The edges gleamed brightly, like frozen sparks caught in the beam.

"Hmmm," agreed Jim. "Amazing how they've stayed intact like that, after all this time, isn't it? I bet old Daedalus had them put there, as part of…" He stopped, and wondered silently.

"Still," Doris said, hopping down off Jim's shoulder and waddling forward across the tiled floor into the gallery, "at least we've got plenty of room to get through between them. Come on, you two."

There *was* plenty of space between the two suspended axes – this gallery was one of the widest that Jim, Doris and Brenda had so far encountered, and if they had been in a truck, they would have been able to drive it through the empty void between the axes.

Doris hop-waddled across the floor, shining her torchbeam at the axes as she approached them.

Jim and Brenda watched Doris. She seemed almost minuscule as she stood between the weaponry.

The archaeologist-poet took out the WINKLIE and

daubed the end against the wall. Then he put it back in his pocket, gave Brenda's mane a quick tousle (to which she fluttered her eyelashes fondly), and followed Doris.

Brenda lifted her head and had a good look at the axes and the walls and the arched doorway at the other end of the gallery. She also noticed, high up on the uneven walls, two narrow slits in the rock – roughly formed apertures, perhaps made by seeping water slowly eroding the rock.

The gallery's silence was broken by only three sounds: Jim's footsteps on the rock floor, Brenda's breath as it sent faint trails of cool vapour from her nostrils, and Doris clucking her tongue against her beak.

"Coo," cooed the macaw when Jim was near her. "They're even bigger when you're up close to them."

Cairo Jim turned to examine the massive weapon hanging opposite the one she was illuminating. "Purely ornamental," he supposed aloud. "They must be. No one would be big enough, or strong enough, to wield such a weapon."

Brenda clop-clopped into the gallery, her torch held firmly between her jaws, her nostrils alert and flared.

"I bet old Bone hasn't been through here yet," Jim said. "He must've turned another corner before he got this far. Why, he'd've probably tried to cut these beauties down and drag them out."

"Scumbag," Doris said, the striped feathers around her beak crinkling with disgust. She turned and continued her hop-waddling through the gallery.

Jim frowned. "But why are they hanging here?"

"Maybe," Doris suggested over her wing, "they were put up as some sort of direction-giver to all those young people when they had to come through this way. You remember, when they had to meet the Minotaur?"

"Maybe," said Jim. He turned and inspected the other axe. At this closer range he could see the fine detail on the carved helve much more clearly. "It seems the ancient Egyptians weren't the only ones who put sharp objects into underground places," he muttered to himself, remembering his encounter with Snip-Hotep's battalion of scissors.

He walked across to the axe and, being very careful, reached out and ran his forefinger gently along the inwards-facing blade. Then he jerked his hand back, and jammed his finger into his mouth.

"Quaaaooo?" snorted Brenda, from the other end of the gallery. She had sensed his panic, and his sudden movement, in the half-lit gloom, even though she was not near him.

"Rark!" Doris screeched from the far end. "What's wrong, Bren?"

Jim took his hand from his mouth and shone his torch onto his finger. "It's nothing, my dear. Nothing, my lovely. I just found out exactly *how* sharp these blades still are."

A tiny dribble of blood welled up on the ball of his finger. He fished out his handkerchief and wrapped it around the cut.

"Are you all right?" Doris squawked.

"Yes, Doris, I'll be fine. It's only a minor cut, really." He hitched his knapsack firmly across his shoulders, pushed back his pith helmet, and walked towards Doris.

"Boys," she clucked. "You always have to touch things..."

Brenda stood still. She shone her torch at her two friends and watched them until Jim had caught up with Doris by the arched doorway at the far end.

When Jim and Doris were together, Brenda began approaching the middle of the gallery and the two axes.

She walked slowly, her senses filling with the underground smell of this place.

She had noticed, with each gallery and corridor and tunnel-like walkway that she had passed through, how the smell in each of the places was always different.

Sometimes a place would smell ancient, that curious sort of ancient smell that Brenda had always thought was like a mixture of damp earth and mildly rotting vegetables. Sour, almost, but not unpleasantly sour. Another place here in the Labyrinth had smelled like old bronze – semi-sweetish, like a trove of forgotten coins that had not seen daylight for a thousand years.

Some corridors had been filled with the aroma of dustiness; some of a strange essence that was a bit like roses; others of shadows (for Brenda, being a Wonder Camel, could smell shadows and their many odours); one of the tunnels had even reminded her of

peppermints, even though there were no peppermints anywhere about.

Occasionally, in the gloom and glimmer, she had detected the faint fragrance of trapped moonlight, which she thought was very strange in such a place so far underground.

As Brenda approached the great pair of hanging axes, her hoofsteps slowed, as her nostrils detected something they had not yet met here in the Labyrinth of Knossos.

Clop-ta-clop-ta-clop.

"Rark! Come on, Bren! We haven't got all day … or night … or whatever … oh, by my beak, it seems like we've been down here so long, I don't even know if it's day or night any more!"

Jim watched as Brenda slowed even more. "My lovely? What is it?"

Now, halfway into the gallery and between the axes, Brenda stopped completely. She raised her head, shining her torch all around the walls, and she opened her nostrils as wide as they could go.

This thing she was smelling for the first time down here, she did not like, for she had sometimes smelt it before, up on the earth: the pure, primeval reek of *fear itself*!

Doris began jerking up and down on the floor. "C'mon, Bren, time's getting on…"

Jim could feel his skin prickling, and he knew that Brenda had detected something. "Brenda, what is it?"

"QUAAAAAOOOOOOOO!" snorted the Wonder Camel, as the next five seconds collapsed in a dizzy heap of terror:

In the floor underneath her, the tiles shifted and two holes appeared, small, black and gaping. Down into these holes slid Brenda's rear hoofs, and she fell helplessly to her knees.

"Reraaaark! Brenda!" Doris screeched and flapped her wings, and Jim took a step forward. But in the next instant they were both frozen with gut-clenching dread.

Swiftly, with barely a sound, the two axes slid across the roof, along an embedded ceiling-track that Jim, Doris and Brenda had not seen in the dimness.

Closer and closer came the axes towards the centre of the gallery.

Brenda saw them moving in. Terrified, she tried to rear up, but her back legs were piped so far under the floor that she could barely raise her front legs.

Her eyes widened, her dark eyeballs darting back and forth, as bucketloads of sweat burst from her humps, splashing down onto the floor all around her.

"Quuaaaaaaooooo!"

"Brenda!" cried Jim. "No! Stay low! Don't try and rear up! The axes, they're—"

There was a loud GRENCHing noise, and both axes slowed. They slowed even more until, with not another sound, they stopped encroaching completely.

Brenda looked to the left and to the right, shining her torch wildly around. The blades of the axes had halted

about three metres on either side of her. In the position that she was stuck in, each of the blades was nearly two metres higher than she.

Seconds passed. Jim watched the axes as they hung there, unmoving but threatening. He took a deep breath, gulped down the Adam's apple of anguish that had risen in his throat, and tried to speak calmly:

"Brenda, now listen carefully. It appears they've stopped whatever they were doing. I'm going to come and get your legs free. Just stay calm and don't make any unnecessary movements. We don't know what might be set off next."

"Stay still, Bren," Doris called, her voice warbling against her will.

"Quaaaooo!" snorted Brenda. She felt the cool, draughty place beneath her, where her back legs were stuck. Slowly, trying to make as little movement as she could, she lowered her torch to the ground, between her front legs, so that its beam was fixed upwards onto the axe to her left.

Jim crouched down and spoke quietly to Doris. "My dear, you keep shining your torch on Brenda. I'll light up the axe on her right. At the slightest movement from either of them, give a screech."

"Rightio."

He stood and took off his knapsack. He pulled out his penknife, flicked open a small shovel-and-pick combination tool from it, and put the knapsack gently on the floor behind Doris.

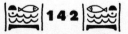

Then, the hairs on his legs standing to attention, he took a step towards the centre of the gallery.

Towards Brenda.

Towards the mighty unknown of the ancient axes.

"REEEEEERAAAAAARKKKKK!" screeched Doris, as if her lungs were about to burst.

Jim flashed his light at the axes, and his blood turned to ice.

Brenda tried to snort, but no sound came.

Silently, with barely a ripple of the cold air, both axes had started to swing back and forth. Out towards the walls their mighty blades arced, up into the dimness, coming a hair's-breadth short of the rock faces.

Then, as the blades were raised high, they fell back in the opposite direction.

Towards Brenda!

Whoooooooooosh!

"Quaaaaoooooo!"

"Brenda!" Jim screamed. "Lower yourself! Down! Down against the floor!"

She gulped in a huge lungful of air and, quick as lightning, collapsed onto the floor.

The blades swung down and in, coming lower with the sweep of their curved path.

Whoooooooooooosh!

Doris and Jim watched, mute, as the blades swept down and crossed each other with hardly a centimetre between them. Brenda felt the hairs on her mane part with the gust of air they made above her, and the

macramé on the uppermost parts of her saddle frayed with the barest contact from the swinging axes.

The massive sharp edges swept upwards, in the opposite directions, once again towards the walls.

"Rark, they're going to come down again!"

The blades hovered for a second close to the walls, and in that second, Jim and Doris saw both axes move two centimetres down on their ceiling rings.

"Oh, no!" Jim panicked. "They're lowering themselves!"

"Bren!" Doris screeched, just as the axes started to fall down and in again, "get as flat against the floor as you possibly can!"

"Quaaaoooo!" She splayed her front legs and hoofs outwards, so that her underbelly could squash closer to the floor.

Jim ran towards her, arriving at her front hoofs just as the axes swung down with a colossal burst of cold air, and crisscrossed directly above Brenda's saddle.

Whoooooooooosh!

"Stay low, my lovely," urged Jim, as the blades swung up to the walls again. "You gained a few more centimetres of clearance that time."

Brenda looked at him, with big, helpless eyes and a trembling lower lip.

Jim scurried around to her rear, to where her legs were trapped, and furiously started attacking the hard floor tiles there with his shovel-and-pick tool.

Doris watched the axes as they arced gracefully

yet sinisterly up to the walls. There they stopped, motionless again.

"They're lowering more!" she cried out. "Another centimetre or two!"

"Quaaaooo!" snorted Brenda, trying to flatten herself even closer to the floor.

"Watch out, Jim! Move back! Here they come again!"

Jim looked up, over his shoulder and then at the opposite wall.

Down came the axes.

"Jim! Get out of the—"

Jim dropped his tool, and half-somersaulted, half-rolled away from Brenda, just as the pair of axes bisected the centre of the gallery.

Whoooooooooooosh!

This time, Brenda felt the sharpness – the icy, zithery trail as the blades sliced further into the top of her macramé saddle. Beneath the woven wool of her camel-blanket, her humps tingled and prickled with heat.

Like a silent ballet of gigantic, non-human dancers, the axes swung back up towards the walls.

Jim crawled quickly back to Brenda. He found the tool and, as he watched the axes pause and lower, he whacked away at the flooring around Brenda's trapped hoofs.

But he stopped when he heard Doris's awful screeching:

"No! Craaaaaaaark! No! They're lowering again, but

not by just a couple of centimetres. They've come down almost half a metre, and – RAAAAAAAAAAAARK!"

Cairo Jim's mouth dropped open. He shone his torch up, watching the axes coming down from the ceiling, the chain attaching them to the rough rock above lengthening, longer and longer, until the weapons were more than half a metre lower than they had been ten seconds before.

His eyes darted to Brenda, to her sides, to her belly, flattened as much as she could be against the cold, hard floor. His hands were dripping with sweat and, before he could help himself, the tool slipped from his fingers, clattering onto the floor tiles.

The axes stopped lowering. Now they were about to curve downwards again.

Brenda shut her eyes and waited for the swift cutting blades to swing towards her.

13

A TWINGE IN JAIPUR

SITTING ON A SHADED, cool terrace in Jaipur, having just returned from a few hours of photograph-taking and shopping at the local antique markets, Jocelyn Osgood put down her Zanskar Thunderer (a fruity drink common in those regions) and thought about her good friend, Jim of Cairo.

The sun was setting slowly over the lush green fields, casting a golden-pinkish hue across the lower part of the sky. Jocelyn stretched out her jodhpurred legs, and in the glow from the fading light, Jim's image also glowed in her subconscious.

She usually found, when she was away on a Valkyrian Airways trip, that this was the time when, without her realising it, her thoughts turned to Jim. She would often wonder what exactly he was up to at that particular moment, so far away from her.

The sun seeped lower behind the hills, and the pinkness turned a dull orange. When the evening sky became tinged with a light greyness, Jocelyn took off her sun-spectacles and pocketed them in the breastpocket of her gaberdine blouse.

She wondered if Jim and Doris and Brenda had been successful in their expedition. Had they found

Bone and his raven? Had they stopped him from ruining another important historical site? Did they have enough to eat? What colour socks was Jim wearing right now?

She sighed and picked up her Zanskar Thunderer, taking a delicate sip through one of the three brightly striped straws. Distance was the hardest thing, she thought to herself. Being so far away.

She didn't mind not being with him half as much when she was in the same country as he, or on the same continent, but when it came to different time zones, and even different days to the ones he was living through, well, she missed him enormously...

Then, quite unexpectedly, a poem that Jim had once written on the back of an envelope, just for her, emerged in her mind. She leaned back, closed her eyes and smiled as she remembered the words:

> Even though we're far apart
> with oceans deep between our hearts,
> and memories come in fits and starts,
> whenever I eat a raspberry tart
> (or anything so sweet),
> whenever I walk along the street
> I'll think of you, my flying friend
> (my other flying friend I mean)
> and my boots will always be clean
> ... and waiting.

It was a funny thing, she told herself, that when she was with Jim, his poetry didn't exactly fill her with gusts of delight. Yet when she was *away* from him, she often warmed at the words he wrote, and—

A shudder, big and unexpected, passed through the entire length of Jocelyn's spine. She sat bolt upright and opened her eyes.

Where had that come from? It definitely wasn't from the Zanskar Thunderer; she had become long ago used to the topsy-turvy effects of those. No, this shudder was something she wasn't used to.

And the fact that she wasn't used to it made her feel very uneasy. It seemed as if this shudder had travelled, had come from somewhere a long distance away…

Jocelyn brushed a hand through her tangly auburn curls and across her brow. Now something just as strange was happening: she could feel a *twinge*, right in the centre of her forehead…

…a twinge of anxiety.

She pressed her fingertips to her forehead and shut her eyes, and an image came to her, an image as bright and as clear as if what was in her mind was before her very eyes.

She had often heard that, when Flight Attendants have been flying for a number of years, they can sometimes experience these strange twinges, which nearly always follow a big, unexpected shudder. It was something to do with the amount of hours spent so

far above the earth, and the changing time-zones they went through.

At Valkyrian Airways, these twinges were known as FATS: Flight Attendants' Twinge Syndrome. She also knew, from several Flight Attendants who had experienced FATS, that these twinges only came when someone close to you was in deep and desperate trouble.

And the twinges were always accompanied by an image that was so realistic, you could have sworn it was there right in front of you, even though you knew it actually wasn't.

The image that was clear in Jocelyn's mind right now, the image that had travelled with this twinge, the image that was almost present right there in front of her, was that of her good friend Cairo Jim. She knew that he, Brenda and Doris were in great trouble.

Jocelyn stood. Her hands had become clammy, and her heartbeat was quick and urgent. Unsteadily, helplessly, she went back to her room in the hotel and tried to sleep.

Sleep did not come.

SHADOW IN THE DARKNESS

BRENDA'S FLANKS were trembling uncontrollably as she lay, sprawled and trapped, in the sweeping path of the gigantic double axes.

Behind her, Jim scrabbled about, trying to find his shovel-and-pick tool. His torchlight shot across the tiled floor, and then upwards, to where the axes were momentarily suspended, motionless.

Doris, at the far end of the gallery, watched the two weapons. Her feathers were drenched with macaw sweat, and her small eyes were brimful with alarm.

Then:

"Raaaark! Here they come!"

Brenda shut her eyes and tried, with all her Wonder Camel might and powers of compression, to get herself closer to the floor. Through her terror, she tried to imagine that she was a part of the floor itself, one of those large, dark tiles, trying to will herself to sink into the surroundings, to be as flat as an envelope.

But she could not get any closer – her humps, under the saddle covering, were still set high.

Jim watched the axes arcing down towards each other. He grabbed Brenda's saddle and pulled her

down with all his strength, until the veins stood out in his neck and perspiration spouted from his temples.

"Be still, my lovely," he tried to soothe. "Be still..."

Whoooooooooooooosh!

Down swept the axes, slicing through the cool, dark air.

Doris buried her head against her chestfeathers. This she could not bear to witness.

Jim rolled out of the way.

Closer the axes came to Brenda, faster now ... speeding, slicing, spearing—

Brenda squirmed and drove her belly hard against the floor, harder than she had ever forced herself in all her life, until she thought she would break the stone tiles and disappear under them.

It was the right move: the squirming repositioned her slightly, just enough to make all the difference.

With a gust of ancient air, the axes crisscrossed right between the Wonder Camel's humps, narrowly clearing the saddle and her backbone beneath it.

"Quaaaoooo!" she snorted with momentary relief.

Doris raised her head. "Bren! You're OK!"

Jim shook his head and quickly crawled back to be with Brenda. As he was crawling, with his torchbeam bobbing this way and that, his hand brushed across his shovel-and-pick tool. He snatched it up and put it to work on the tiles around Brenda's rear hoofs.

"Stay still, my lovely. I'll have you out in three shakes of a camel's—"

"Hurry!" screeched Doris. "Look! The axes are descending even further!"

Jim shone his torch up to one of the axes. He and Brenda watched, their skin and hair crawling, as it lowered another metre.

Cairo Jim felt his heart go brick-heavy, and he found his senses slowing, numbing, with the awful realisation that at that distance from the ceiling, both axes would sweep through the centre of the gallery with a clearance space of only a few centimetres from the floor.

Brenda had been thinking the same thing – in fact, her realisation of the matter reached Jim and Doris in a flash of a second. She knew that unless she or Jim could get her legs out of those holes, this would be the end.

Doris watched the axes, her beak aquiver, her feathers standing on end. "They're ... they're swinging. They're starting to..." Her little voice trailed off; she could not bear to speak another squawk.

Down, like a mighty set of sharp, lethal fists, swung the ancient axes. In the torchlight, their blades glinted with diabolical silver and gold.

And Cairo Jim made a decision: there would be about five seconds before they reached Brenda. Not enough time for him to free her hoofs. But enough time for him to try to spare her, or at least lessen the damage to her.

The archaeologist-poet took a big gulp and stood. He moved fast, faster than he'd ever moved, leaping up

onto Brenda's saddle and sitting atop her with his legs astride his noble friend.

Doris screeched loud enough to wake the dead: "Jim! Noooooooooooo!"

Brenda rolled her head and saw where he was. Her heart flooded with something, a huge, warm but sad sensation, as she realised the sacrifice he was about to make.

Down continued the axes…

WHOOOOOOOOOOOOSH!

Cairo Jim pushed back his pith helmet and sat erect. In another two seconds…

And then, as Brenda wriggled, trying to get free, and as Doris was about to lift her wings and fly to be with her friends in this, the final seconds of their friendship, there was a flicker in the shadows.

It was way up, behind one of the slit-holes high on the walls, in the darkness there. A different sort of darkness, not as dense. Brenda glimpsed it out of the corner of her eye, and speared her torchlight towards the hole.

From behind the slit, in the blink of a nano-second, there was a flash of flame.

It came.

A moment.

Gone.

Then, just as the axes were about to bisect each other's path and to strike Jim of Cairo sharply against his sides, to cut through him as if he were a mound

of butter, there came a great grinding, like the earth waking up after a long, long sleep, and then stretching, splitting itself at its seams.

GRHHHHHHEENNNNNNNNNNNNKKKKKKK HHHHHHHHHKKKKK!

And the axes stopped swinging…

…Two and a half centimetres on each side of Jim's trembling shoulders.

"What the—?" gasped Jim, looking wildly around.

"Quaaaooo?"

"I'll be flapped!" blurted Doris, dropping her torch. Quickly she scooped it up again and watched, her chest heaving, as the axes began silently rising to the ceiling.

Jim watched them, too, his breath coming like a shy and timid visitor to his lungs.

Brenda held her torch in her shaking jaws. She raised her head and saw the axes returning to their original positions.

There was a loud CLUNKing sound, and the axes locked back into place.

"Quaaaoooo," Brenda snorted excitedly. The holes around her hoofs had got bigger! With a bound and a lurch, she pulled in her front legs, extended them beneath her, and then almost leapt up out of the holes.

Jim had to hold onto her saddle tightly. "Whoa, my lovely, lovely Brenda!" he cried, half laughing and half crying.

Doris flew to them, her torch in her claws, and landed on Brenda's head. "I think I need a change of

feathers after that little incident," she squawked. "Why did the axes stop?"

"I've no idea," said Jim. "And we don't want to hang around to find out. Let's get out of here!" He jumped down from the saddle and took Brenda's reins in his hand. "Out of this gallery altogether."

As Jim led her to the doorway, Brenda looked up, high up the wall to the slit-like hole. All that she could *see* behind it now was blackness – thick, gloomy, nothing-more-than-this-now-or-ever blackness.

But the Wonder Camel *knew* otherwise.

15

GLOOM WITH A VIEW

AFTER THEIR ENCOUNTER with the axes, Jim, Doris and Brenda decided to rest. They reasoned that it was probably night up on the earth … they couldn't be exactly sure, because when Jim went to check the time, he found that his Cutterscrog Old Timers Archaeological Timepiece had stopped, and no matter how much he wound it, it wouldn't start again.

They found another cavernous room at the end of another corridor. At the far end of the room was another arched doorway, leading further into the Labyrinth. The left-hand wall of the room was sheer, glistening, and black-as-pitch; the wall opposite was only a half-wall, no higher than Jim's waist.

"Looks like a good place to bed down," he said, jumping from Brenda's saddle, and nearly skidding on the smooth rock floor.

"Rark," Doris rarked. She flew down onto the ledge of the half-wall and peered over, casting her torchbeam downwards. "Well, get a squizz at this," she said quietly.

Jim and Brenda came over and looked down, shining their torches into the void below.

Far beneath them, the floor glittered and moved, silently and smoothly.

"Water," said Jim. He moved his beam across the glittering, dark surface. "A huge underground river."

"Coo."

"Quaaooo."

He reached down, picked up a small rock from the floor, and tossed it gracefully over the ledge.

Ten seconds later, they heard a faint splash and *ploop* sound.

A smile spread across Jim's face. "Let's get our collapsible bucket and rope and haul up some water. I think I'd like a good cup of tea before sleep."

Which is exactly what they did.

After they had lit their kerosene lamp and had made tea, and then set up Jim's bedding and Doris's makeshift portable perch and Brenda's sleeping mat, and when they had finished a meal of tinned snails, freeze-dried worms and Poshoglian's Canned Spatchcock with Plums and Artichoke Hearts (Gerald Perry Esquire had adventurous ideas when it came to supplying provisions for Cairo Jim), sleep came quickly to Jim and Doris.

Brenda, though, did not sleep. She still had so much excitement pulsating through her humps and flanks and hoofs that she remained wide awake. She did not mind this, however; being a Wonder Camel, she usually relied on very little sleep, and besides, tonight she preferred to keep a watch on things while her friends slept.

And to maybe see that shadow and its lick of flame again...

★ ★ ★

"I think," announced Neptune Flannelbottom Bone, "that we shall stop here for the night. I need to get some rest before the continuation of my quest for Greatness."

He put down his candle and stretched his flabby arms wide and had a yawn, his bearded mouth gaping like a hairy cave. Then he took a roll of tatty blanket from the little wagon, spread it on the floor and plonked his substantial body down upon it. "Arrrr."

"Eh?" asked Desdemona, her eyes throbbing. "Whaddya mean, stop here for the night? Aren't we gonna go back up to our cave?"

"You heard me, grumbleguts. We stay *here* this evening." He took off his fez and placed it on the blanket next to him.

She slung off the little wagon and rolled her shoulder blades, opening her wings and closing them. "Why? Every other night we've gone out again. Back up to the land of the livin'. Why're we stayin' down here tonight?"

He leant on an elbow and stretched out his legs (the embroidered faces of several Australian Prime Ministers on his plus fours warped and distorted in the most unfortunate ways).

"Well?" she rasped. "You gonna answer me, or should I just keep myself company?"

Bone sighed loudly. "Because, you detestable dredged-up dumkopf, you may not have noticed it, but in the last twenty-four hours or so, we have come far deeper into this underground maze, into this dank

dominion of dinginess, than we have on any other day so far."

"So what?" She hopped up and down, trying to get some blood flowing through her cold body.

"So, we would be wasting valuable time going out and then coming in again tomorrow morning. Look around you, Desdemona. You yourself said that the walls have been changing."

She raised an eyeball, and the candle that was stuck to the top of her head cast a crazy flicker onto the wall. "Yeah, everything's gettin' darker."

"And bigger," added Bone, lighting a Belch of Brouhaha cigar and letting the smoke curl through his beard. "These caverns, never visited by man, woman, child or beast in thousands of years, are now huge enough to contain that which I seek. The great Talos himself."

Desdemona eyeballed him as he replaced his silver cigar-lighter in a pocket of his emerald-green waistcoat. "Talos, Talos, Talos," she grumbled. "You and your dream schemes. The best laid plans of whales and men..."

He blew a shaft of foul smoke straight at her. "Enshut your beak and be silent. I need rest now, to rekindle my ambition and my natural instinctive traits."

"Y'can keep yer stinky traits to yerself," she croaked under her breath. With a hop and a limp, she went and found a bit of floor that wasn't as damp as the rest, and tried to make herself as comfortable as she could for the night.

Bone stretched himself out fully, his wide back

completely covering the blanket. He stared up at the far-off ceiling, at what he could see of it lit up by Desdemona's feeble candle flame.

It was the dark to end all darkness up there, and the fleshy man felt a surge of solidarity: he knew what darkness meant, and what safety it held, not only so high above, but also so deep within.

"Greater than Zeus Himself," he mumbled, his eyes closing and his cigar falling from his fingers and slowly extinguishing against the cold floor. "Greater than Zeus Him … zzzzzzzzz … "

Nine hours and fourteen minutes later, Bone was awakened from a dream – a pleasant dream that had involved Joan Crawford and himself and a rare Great Mongolian Horse-head Fiddle – by a persistent bouncing on his chest.

"Scrark!" scrarked Desdemona, using this part of his anatomy as a makeshift trampoline. "Rise and whine, oh slumbering mountain of Genius!"

"Arrrrr, what in the name of decency?" He opened one flabby eyelid and saw the scrofulous bird, her rough yellow tongue hanging out of her beak as she bounced up and down with great enthusiasm.

"I'm your early mornin' wake-up call. You've been snorin' for ages, and it's been makin' me fleas bite even harder. They don't like the reverbaratio. Ouch!" She stopped bouncing and pecked at a dozen fleas attacking her underwing.

"Get off, you atrocious alarm clock of awfulness!" He swept her harshly to the floor with the back of his hand, and sat up groggily.

"Oooof!" she grunted. She rolled over and sprang to her talons. Her head-candle had long ago gone out, and her sudden fall from Bone's stomach had loosened the wax that attached it to her feathers. She reached up and pulled it off.

"Get me some bread rolls from the little wagon," he ordered her.

"Yeah, yeah, yeah." She hopped to the little wagon and pulled out six rolls wrapped in greaseproof paper. These she threw at the blanket, one by one.

"And replace those candles on the little wagon. As you can see, they've almost burnt down to nothing!"

"Slave driver," she muttered, but she did as she had been told, while Bone busied himself with the bread rolls. Earlier, while Bone had been sleeping, she had finished her last tin of Japanese seaweed.

Soon all the rolls had been devoured, and Bone wiped the crumbs from his beard with the back of his hand.

"Now I understand what humans mean when they talk about landfill," thought the raven, watching him silently.

"Right," said Bone, putting his fez on his greasy hair and standing. "Onwards into the maze. Harness yourself, and—"

A low, muffled moaning – or a sound something like

moaning, for it was hard to tell what sounds really were, with all the thick rock walls down here – washed through the tunnels ahead.

"Oooooouuuuuuuggghhhhhh…"

"Listen," croaked Desdemona. "Whassat?"

Bone raised his head. The sound grew deeper and louder, then softer, then deeper and louder again.

Then it faded away, leaving a heavy, damp silence.

"Sounded like an ocean," said Desdemona, her feathers starting to hackle uncomfortably. "Like waves comin' and goin' out on the sand." She looked confused. "But on the other claw, it doesn't sound like water." She shook her beak. "Hmmm. I've heard that sound before…"

A huge surge of excitement tore through every pore in Bone's hide. "Quickly, my foul, fetid fiend, come here so that I may fix your skull-candle. We must be on our way. I have an almost touchable feeling that my search will be fulfilled in just a matter of corridors! Oh, the power, the power! Arrrrr!"

Many tunnels westward, Cairo Jim, Doris and Brenda had also awoken.

Their night had been quiet, and without incident. Jim and Doris had slept soundly, both of them only waking every couple of hours to check that Brenda was all right.

The vigilant Wonder Camel had kept an eye on the night and the cavernous room overlooking the river so

 **163**

far below. She had calmly meditated and pondered, replenishing the reserves of strength and fortitude and clear-snoutedness within her, as she had kept watch.

Now, Jim, Doris and Brenda felt almost fully refreshed and ready to continue their journey. After a small breakfast of snails, freeze-dried worms and a can of Poshoglian's Hibiscus-Flavoured Oatmeal and Brussels Sprouts with Coriander Leaves (Jim had made a mental note to have a word with Perry when they got back about Perry's choice of tinned foods), they packed up their night equipment and set off once more.

For nearly five hours they passed through corridors and tunnels and rooms that were cavernous and almost unimaginably vast.

On and on ... and on...

Jim led the way, his torchlight darting across the walls and doorways, the arches and steps (for many times the trio found themselves descending stairways – sometimes long, narrow stairways on which Brenda especially had to be extremely careful where she placed her hoofs, and sometimes wide, roughly hewn sets of no more than a dozen steps that would lead them down into a new chamber).

Doris alternated where she travelled. Often she would ride on Jim's shoulder, or on the crown of his pith helmet. At other times she would fly ahead a little, stopping on the ground and beckoning Jim and Brenda onwards with an impatient yet caring wave of her

beautiful yellow-and-blue wing. And at other times she would ride on Brenda – on her head (between her ears) or on the pommel of her saddle or on one of her macramé-covered humps.

Jim, Doris and Brenda descended deeper and deeper, further and further, into this intricate and dizzyingly confusing maze...

Hours passed. Then, after countless corridors and steps and tunnel-like chambers, they were about to turn a sharp corner. Jim whipped out his WINKLIE and daubed it against the rock wall, and then put it away again (his WINKLIE, not the rock wall – his pockets were not that capacious).

While he was doing this, Doris hop-fluttered from his shoulder to the floor. She waddled around the corner, shining her torch into the depth of gloom ahead.

And she screeched like she had not screeched in a long, long time.

"CRAAAAAAAAAAARAAAAAAAAAAARAAAAAAAA AAAREEEEEEEERAAAAAAARKKKKKKKKKK!"

Jim jumped, as did Brenda, high into the air, as the echo of her screech shot into their ears and spines (and other places where, before this, Jim and Brenda had never imagined that sound could enter).

"D ... Doris," stammered the archaeologist-poet, hurtling around the corner, his heart pumping at a thousand miles per second. "What—?"

"Quaaaaaaooooo?" Brenda, too, charged around the narrow turn.

When they saw what lay ahead, they, like Doris, froze in silence.

They were standing at the edge of a high and narrow antechamber, the walls of which were blacker than a starless, winter's night. At the opposite end, another doorway led further into the Labyrinth. This doorway was festooned with a thick curtain of faintly billowing cobwebs, silvery and dust-laced, ancient and long-ago abandoned.

But it was not the cobwebs that had stopped the trio in their tracks. It was what lay between them and the cobwebs.

As their torchlights scanned the floor of the antechamber, they saw that it was littered with bones and skulls – the yellowish, dry, brittle-looking remains of human beings.

Most of the skeletons were lying intact on the floor, in positions which suggested that they had come to rest there and had not been disturbed since the time they had been placed there – or had lain themselves down when they had been alive.

Some of the skeletons still had traces of clothing attached: a piece of leather tunic here, a stiff fragment of linen there. A few were wearing what looked like gold bracelets on their wrist bones, and ornaments that might have once been silver or gold necklaces or diadems around their neck bones.

The eye sockets of the skulls stared up, vacant, hollow, grey with the neglect of this forgotten tomb.

The remaining teeth grinned strangely in the torchlight.

"Swoggle me sepulchrely," said Jim.

"This," said Doris, "is one part of our job I could gladly leave behind."

"Quaaaooo quaaaooo," agreed Brenda, although she was mildly fascinated with what she and her friends had discovered. Jim pushed his pith helmet back, and frowned. "They … they must be … must've *been* … some of the young people sent down here for the Minotaur…"

"What a way to go," Doris squawked.

"Although," thought Brenda, "they don't appear to have physically suffered. From the way they're lying there, it seems they had gentle deaths."

"Although," Jim said, tapping his chin with his index finger, "they don't appear to have physically suffered. From the way they're lying there, it seems they had gentle deaths. Not the violent endings we've come to know about."

Doris shivered. "Rark! Let's make our way through them and get to what lies beyond!"

"In a few minutes, my dear." Jim unslung his knapsack and took out his notebook. "I need to take some notes, so that we can record all of this. Then maybe a future expedition can relocate it all."

"Of course," said Doris, blinking.

For fifteen minutes, Jim moved through the antechamber and jotted down the findings, embellishing the descriptions with small drawings of the jewellery and ornaments worn by the skeletons.

He had just finished, and was slipping his pencil back into the loop on the side of the notebook, and putting the notebook back in his knapsack, when a low, wave-like sound seeped through the walls.

Doris, perched on Brenda's pommel, looked up.

Brenda's ears twitched, and she opened her long eyelashes wide.

Jim felt the hairs on the back of his legs, behind his kneecaps, stand on end.

"Oooooouuuuuuuggghhhhhh…"

The sound continued, swelling louder and then receding until it was as faint as the sound of air itself.

Then it was gone completely.

"Must be the wind," Jim said, but he didn't seem quite convinced.

"Undoubtedly," agreed Doris, but she was even less sure.

"Quaaaooo," snorted Brenda, but she kept her thoughts to herself, locked away, until she could be more certain.

"Come on, then." Jim hitched his knapsack over his shoulders and picked his way through the skeletons to the cobwebbed doorway. "Let's find Neptune Bone!"

ALMIGHTY CLANGER

THE OBESE MAN whose lower regions were adorned with the faces of all the Prime Ministers of Australia padded quietly around a curved wall, his candle held above his fez.

"Heavens to the Goddess Betsy," he gasped, stopping suddenly.

Desdemona, bringing up the rear and the little wagon, banged into Sir Earle Page and William Morris Hughes. "Oof," she grunted.

"Ouch!" shrieked Bone, rubbing the backs of his thighs. "Watch where you're shoving that beak!"

She looked up at him coldly, her eyes throbbing with tiredness and mild malevolence. "Well, if you didn't go stoppin' all of a sodden, ya wouldn't have ta worry. What's the hold-up, anyway?"

Bone grabbed her by her wing and pulled her roughly forward. "Behold, you untrusting urk of ugliness. Behold … *the final chamber*!"

Desdemona shook off his pudgy hand and squinted ahead.

Before them lay the biggest chamber they had so far encountered. It was unfathomably vast, its walls almost mirror-black and so reflective that the dozen candles

on the little wagon and on Desdemona's head and in Bone's hand were multiplied in their reflections so that it looked like a million candles were glowing.

"It's like … they've got electricity down here," stammered the raven.

"Fitting," said Bone, "that my moment of the Getting of Unconquerable Power should be thus illuminated."

"It's lit up for ya, as well."

Bone raised his candle higher, and the reflections cast the light further upwards. The brightness crept up the black mirror walls, gradually revealing the ceiling: a wide, vaulted structure carved from the very glistening rock itself.

"Arrrr," moaned Neptune Bone. "This must be the place, Desdemona, it *must* be! That ceiling, these walls … there has not been another place in all of this Labyrinth so beautifully and completely built."

Desdemona pecked at a flea on her pot-belly and spat it onto the floor.

"I am certain," Bone continued, "that Daedalus took great care with this chamber, on the orders of King Minos. After all, Minos would not have wanted to put so precious and valuable a power as Talos into a cold, wet pit, would he?"

"Search me."

Bone became very still, as a steam-train surge of goosebumps consumed his flesh, rushing, spreading, *riddling* over his skin (which was always affected this way whenever he believed he was standing on the

doorstep of amazing opportunity). "Oh, raven, I am having one of those moments of pure Genius again … oh, it is taking over my being … *arrrrrrrrr*!"

Desdemona hopped quickly aside (the little wagon bumping behind her) in case things got nasty.

"This," he whispered, when the goosebumps began to subside, "will be known as the crowning moment of Neptune Flannelbottom Bone, and in the future—"

"Well, fondue me follicles!" Desdemona croaked loudly.

"What? How dare you interrupt me, you rude—"

"Look, you old windbag! Look what I can see!"

Bone glared at her eyeballs, which appeared to be throbbing with a sort of hot curiosity. Slowly he followed the path of where she was looking.

When Desdemona had jumped aside, she had cast the light from her candle, and the candles on the little wagon, into a new part of the chamber – an annex that opened out into a longer, even more grandiose area.

Here, at the edge of this annex, Bone saw what Desdemona had seen…

…it was facing away from them, and it was massive.

"Come, raven!" he hissed. "Come, come, come!"

Boldly he strode forward, through the grand gallery, towards the annex, his candlelight multiplying on the walls as he proceeded, like a walking whale surrounded by a moving tide of brightness.

Desdemona followed in his wake, all of her candles lighting up the place a million-fold.

Bone came to the edge of the annex and stopped, his eyes big, his belly heaving with excitement. The thing he'd seen was almost as tall as his shoulders. And he knew exactly what it was.

Unlike Desdemona.

"Well?" she asked when she had caught up. "What is it?"

"Can't you tell?" he whispered, his beard bristling.

She looked up at the rounded, rigid thing. "Nope. It's just an enormous bit of … thing."

Bone turned slowly to his left and walked a few steps. The candlelight reflected along the walls and swelled all around him. "Look, there's another one."

Desdemona saw it: another rounded, rigid thing, just like the first. On this one, from where she was standing, she could also see a little protuberance, like a softened triangle, bulging out near the round bit at the back.

Bone looked up, holding the candle higher. "Well spiflicate my globules," he said, whistling.

"Tell me, what is it? Put me out of me mystery."

"I'll do better than that, you dim dreg of dinginess. I shall *show* you what it is!"

She squinted at him, watching carefully as he went forward and disappeared down some stairs that she had not noticed before between the two objects.

"Hey, wait for me!" After him she rushed, the little wagon bumping and banging as it descended the stairs.

Now Bone was in the grandest of the chambers, and he was hurrying up the centre of it, not looking back.

Desdemona hop-flutter-scurried after him.

The little wagon lurched and teetered after her, its candles bright and brilliant against the glassy walls of the chamber.

Then, when Bone felt he was in the very centre of the chamber, he turned, his eyes downcast to the floor. "Do the same as I, Desdemona ... keep your eyes averted when you turn, and I promise you a sight that you will never forget ... a sight that you will recall when you think the world has lost all its marvel and appeal and excitement, and which will remind you that treasures lie where you least suspect!"

She came to his side, turned, and kept her eyeballs fixed on the floor.

"Now," he whispered, his voice higher pitched than usual, "when I give the word, raise your eyes and behold. One."

"One," she repeated.

"Two." His breathing was getting quicker.

"Two," she repeated.

"Three! Look now!"

"Eh?" she said, because counting was always something she had trouble with, and she thought that eight came next. Or maybe it was six.

"Look, bird, look!"

Together, they raised their eyes. Slowly, slowly, silently, up and up.

First they saw two enormous feet, dusty but yellowish-orange, shining in places but dull elsewhere. Each of the feet had a sandal strapped across it, made of the same metal as the feet.

"Tootsies!" gasped Desdemona. "We was lookin' at the backs of two tootsies! Now I get it … them things before were the heels, only they was too big for me ta realise … and I saw an ankle, and—"

"Look to whom they belong!"

The feet were attached to a pair of towering bronze legs, each as wide as three men standing shoulder to shoulder. The legs stretched far up into the grand chamber.

"Hello, Big Boy," gasped Bone.

"Hoo hoo hoo," rasped Desdemona.

"May I introduce you," Bone said to her, with mock courtesy, "to my new associate. Talos the Obedient. Protector of Neptune F. Bone, and Servant of his Brilliance. Our search is at an end. *Arrrrrr!*"

For once, the raven forgot all about her fleas.

There, bathed in myriad reflected candlelight, silent and hulking, its legs astride the staircase that Bone and Desdemona had descended, stood the mighty ancient bronze statue itself, motionless, waiting…

Bone and Desdemona craned their necks, higher and higher. Their gaze panned upwards, over the bronze tunic that hung over Talos' body, past the waist and chest, to the shoulders, as broad as a truck is wide.

One of the mighty arms of Talos hung by the statue's

side; the other was raised, bent at the rippling elbow, and was holding a long, sharp sword, the size of which gave Bone's knees a tremor.

Then there was the face.

"I need to see his features," Bone said. "Come here!"

"Who, me?" asked Desdemona.

"No, I mean Mama Cass. Who d'you think I mean?" He crouched down and pulled the raven close to him.

"What're you—?"

"There." Bone had unhitched the little wagon's harness from her wings. "Now, with your skull-candle on your head, fly up to the ceiling and flutter all around his face. The light will be magnified against the walls and I shall be able to look upon his visage."

"Me?" she protested. "Me fly up *near* that thing?"

"Well I'd do it myself, but my wings are at the dry-cleaners. Hurry up, you frittering felonious fool."

"No way, Desiree. I ain't goin' near him. What if he suddenly comes to life? He could bat me inta Kingdom Come with a blink of his eyelids! He could suck me inta his nostril with a single breath! He could burp and blow me inta the middle of next month! He could—"

"And I could pluck every feather from your body and hand your pink little carcass over to the Antiquities Squad in an anonymous package." He brought his face close to hers and she saw fires she had never seen before, far into his eyes. *"Are you going to disobey me?"*

The threat hung like lead curtains around her. She looked away from his fires and up at the faraway,

shadowy face of Talos. The thought of the Antiquities Squad seeing her naked was a fate she, nor any raven, would ever want. And besides, she thought, if Talos *did* decide to come to life and to chase after her, she could probably fly faster than Talos could walk.

"All right, all right, all right. You win."

"I knew you'd see things my way." Bone picked her up by the neck, stood, and, being careful that her skull-candle didn't extinguish, hurled her towards the vaulted ceiling.

"Yeeeerrrrgghhh," she cried as she shot helplessly into the air.

Bone watched her as she found her airborne balance and flapped her way towards Talos' head.

As she came closer, her candlelight increased a thousandfold against the mirrored walls. Within seconds, Bone could see all.

"Look!" he exclaimed. "See his features? They are almost … almost human!"

"*Too* almost human," Desdemona muttered, scowling, as she hovered in front of the head. "Specially from this close!"

The face of Talos was as big as a car with all its doors open. He had no beard, but a fine, exposed chin, with a strong, determined jawline. His nose was aquiline, his bronze cheekbones high. The brow was wide and smooth, and on the very top of his head there was a covering of tightly formed bronze curls.

The eyes of this awesome statue were both closed.

Like the limbs, there was no sign of life.

Desdemona flew back and forth, casting angles of light across Talos' face and neck and upper shoulders. She never took her eyes off Talos' closed eyelids.

"Oh, Mr Genius?" she called.

Bone, who had been transfixed by the handsomeness and physique of Talos, blinked. "What do you want?" he shouted, his growling voice echoing.

"I have a question."

"Ask, and ye shall be enlightened."

"How do you get it ta come ta life and obey you?"

"Well, that's simple. All I have to do is…" His voice trailed off. "What did you say?"

"I said, how're you gonna get it started? Does it come with instructions or a manual book?"

Bone slowly reached up and removed his fez. He scratched the top of his hair with his index finger. He realised, as if a bolt of lightning had just hit him squarely in the back, that when he had been down in the Underworld, when he had heard whisper of the existence of Talos in the Labyrinth of King Minos, he had not heard an additional piece of vital information – how Talos could be resurrected.

The lip of the fleshy man curled. How, he thought, could those things in the Underworld, those things that had told him of Talos, how could they have been so *stupid* to leave out this vital information?

Did they not know that he, Neptune Flannelbottom Bone, did not have all the time under the world to

waste? Why, oh why, could they not have been more informative?

"Well?" called Desdemona. "How?"

"I have my methods," he shouted back, his cheeks flushed with anger.

"Yeah," rasped the raven. "And I'm Amy Johnson out ta break aviation history!"

Bone kicked at a piece of rock on the floor. "Arrrr," he muttered bitterly.

Desdemona kept hovering, watching him as Bone began to stride back and forth, his hands clasped angrily behind his back.

There must be a way, he thought anxiously. It must be obvious to a man of my unsurpassable intellect. I just have to hit upon it.

"Hey," scrarked the raven. "Me wings are gettin' tired!"

Bone ignored her and kept pacing. Maybe, he thought, there is some ancient Greek incantation that needs to be uttered? He snarled quietly as he remembered that if that were the case, he would not be able to supply it; he had wagged most of his Ancient Greek Incantations of Mythology classes way back when he was a student at Archaeology School. He had had better things to do at the time, like swindling tourists at the Giza Pyramids and attending a certain burlesque theatre where there was an interesting act that featured an octopus who played the trombone.

"Hey, wobbleboy!" Desdemona called. "I said, me wings are tirin'!"

Still Bone ignored her, as he continued pacing and thinking. Perhaps there was some sort of opening somewhere on the surface of Talos? After all, Bone did remember that the statue was supposed to be able to come alive because of a liquid that ran throughout its entire body along a single vein…

"Arrrr," he arrrred. That must be it! He stopped pacing and turned to face Talos again.

"Well," squawked the raven, "if you ain't gonna even bother to answer me, see if I care." She looked at Talos and decided that Bone probably had no way of getting the statue animated.

So, with her eyes throbbing redly, she fluttered down and came to land on Talos' mighty shoulder.

The shoulder with the raised arm, holding the sword.

There was a creaking – a high-pitched shifting of metal and grit and something unknown and ancient. It grew louder and higher, filling every corner of the grand chamber, swelling like a tidal wave of discordant uproar.

"SCREEEEEEEEEEEEEEEEEEEEUUUUUUUUU UWWWWWWCCCCCCKKKKKKKKKK!"

Bone clamped his hands hard over his ears. "Oh, the grating! My ears, my ears! What is—?"

And, just around the corner, the awful din was heard by others.

❖❖❖❖❖ **17** ❖❖❖❖❖

HOW THE MIGHTY
HAVE FALLEN

"SWOGGLE ME SCREECHILY!" cried Cairo Jim. "What was that?"

"Rark! It came from around that corner!"

"Quaaaooo," snorted Brenda, in her most urgent let's-hurry-and-find-out tone.

Jim, with Doris on his shoulder, raced down the sloping floor of the tunnel they were in, with Brenda galloping right behind.

When they turned the corner, they came to a dead-stop.

And each of them sucked the air into their lungs, totally amazed, as their eyes adjusted to the bright magnification of the candles and torchlights and what lay before them.

They had entered the grand chamber from the front. There, halfway into the chamber, with his back to them and his hands pressed firmly against his ears, was the unmistakable figure of Neptune Bone.

The eyes of Jim, Doris and Brenda took in his shape, and then moved further on, to the opposite end of the grand gallery.

When they each beheld the towering figure of Talos, their three hearts began to beat so fast that for a moment

the three of them felt dizzy, and the scene in front of them spun around in circles before their eyes.

Jim shook his head, Doris blinked and Brenda swished her tail through the cool air. Their dizziness vanished.

But now the dreadful scraping noise, the awful creaking of bronze and twisting of metal resumed:

"SCREEEEEEEEEEEEUUUUUUUUUWWWW CCCCCCKKKKKKKKKK!"

Jim winced, and Doris and Brenda shuddered at the grating, awful commotion.

Ahead of them, Bone sank to his knees, as the sound made him weaken. "Arrrr, this is detestable. Worse than a million cats being mangled!"

Desdemona, still on Talos' shoulder, suddenly felt her world moving.

"Scraaaark! No! The statue! It's—"

Bone watched, horror-stuck, as Talos teetered slowly forwards, creaking louder than ever.

"Oh, no," Jim gasped above the sound of twisting bronze. "Talos is ... falling!"

"Craaarkkk!" screeched Doris.

"Quaaaaaoooo!" snorted Brenda.

"You stupid raven," Bone shouted, shaking his fist. "You made it overbalance!"

"Let me off!" wailed Desdemona, flying well away from the swaying statue.

Forwards it lurched, then backwards a little. With each movement the din got louder and more ear-piercing.

"SCREEEEEEEEEEEEUUUUUUUUUWWWW WCCCCCCKKKKKKKKKK!"

As it lurched forward again, the arm holding the sword tore loose from the shoulder with a jagged thunderclap of torn and twisted metal.

"ARRRRRRRRRR!" wailed Bone, on his knees and cowering.

Down crashed the arm and sword, clattering against the floor with a noise loud enough to shake the foundations of Knossos Palace, so far above.

Jim, Doris and Brenda screwed their eyes tightly shut, and covered their ears even more densely with their hands and wings and, in Brenda's case, with her unique ear-protection muscles.

"SCREEEEEEEEEEEEUUUUUUUUUWWWW WCCCCCCKKKKKKKKKK!"

Now Talos swayed back. The left leg slid across the stone platform, next to the steps, with an agonising SCRENCH.

As Talos came teetering forwards again, his centre of balance finally deserted him. Down he started to plunge, into the centre of the grand chamber.

Jim saw that Bone, cowering with his face to the floor, was in the direct line of Talos' fall. If Bone didn't get out of the way, he would be crushed by the tonnes of ancient bronze.

Without thinking, Cairo Jim threw off his pith helmet, raced into the middle of the chamber, dived at Bone, and shunted him towards the side wall.

"Oooof!" grunted the obese man, rolling along the floor.

"CRARK!" Doris screeched, almost fretting out of her feathers, "Jim, watch out! Here he—"

Jim, still in the centre of the chamber, rolled over, shook his head sharply, and looked back over his shoulder. His eyes bulged with panic.

Talos was almost on top of him, falling, falling, gleaming with his hurtling weight…

With not a second to think, Jim flattened himself on the floor and rolled, so fast that he was a blur against the stone tiles. Over and over and over he rolled, until he banged against the opposite side wall.

All of Talos' towering height and bronze muscles crashed down onto the floor with the most colossal smashing sound ever heard by human, macaw, Wonder Camel or raven, and a great cloud of dust rose up, blasting all the way to the vaulted ceiling.

The ground shook, as if an enormous earthquake had struck.

It took ten minutes for the dust to subside, and for the ringing in the ears of all present to gradually fade away.

When everyone had finished coughing, and had got their breath back, Bone stood and glowered at the fallen statue. The once invincible Talos now lay, smashed into hundreds of pieces of mangled, crushed bronze.

"You stupid raven," muttered the fleshy, dishevelled man, not to Desdemona, but to the mess in front of him.

High above, on one of the buttresses in the ceiling, Desdemona perched, her dark feathers partially camouflaging her against the black, glistening roof.

Doris and Brenda came to Jim. "Are you all right?" asked the macaw.

"Fine," puffed the archaeologist-poet, brushing himself down. "Just a few bruises, I think."

"Quaaaaooo," snorted Brenda, rolling her head with relief.

Bone was still muttering. "All my dreams, resting on the shoulders of one so lifeless. Arrrr, if only I could have got you moving again, before that wretched wraith of wrongness went and caused you to fall…"

Jim, Doris and Brenda watched him across the remains of Talos.

"He's dazed," Doris said.

"Quaaooo," agreed Brenda.

Jim stepped towards the wreckage and picked up his pith helmet. In a loud voice, he called Bone's name.

Bone blinked, and his head shot up. He peered at the ceiling, trying to pick out Desdemona among all the gloom.

"What do you want, you eternally stupid bird?" he snarled. "You colossally clumsy clump of—"

"Crark! Wasn't me. It was him!"

For a moment, Bone looked confused. Then he lowered his gaze, and squinted, through the last veil of the settling dust, across the ruined Talos.

And his eyes set on Jim, Doris and Brenda.

"ARRRRRR. What the deuce are you lot doing here?"

Doris, sitting on Brenda's head and unable to contain her anger at Bone's ingratitude any longer, puffed out her chestfeathers and let out an almighty screech.

"*Reeeeeeeeraaaaaaaaark!* You miserable, over-inflated windbag! If it wasn't for Jim of Cairo, you would've been crushed to smithereens under all of this!"

"Wretched goody-goodies," croaked Desdemona, high above.

"I think not," snarled the fleshy man.

"I think SO," Doris remonstrated. "Jim rushed at you and pushed you out of the way. A few seconds later and it would've been goodbye Neptune Bone and hello strawberry jam!"

"Arrrr." Bone shook his head slowly ... he could not recall anything that had happened after the awful din of Talos' creaking reached its crescendo.

"By the way," Doris added, eyeing the gaudy array of solemn faces all over Bone's lower abdomen and legs, "that's a particularly nasty pair of plus fours you're wearing."

Brenda shuddered at the sight.

Jim gestured at the bits of smashed bronze. "So, Bone, is this what you were after?"

"You ignorant moron," Bone answered. "You in your snazzy piffle helmet. You came here to thwart me, and you think you have succeeded."

"We came here," said Jim, taking another step forward, "to stop any plunder. When we found out you were sniffing about here under Knossos, we knew we had to come."

"You posturing pathetic *poet*. I am sure your mother was frightened by a typewriter, or concussed by a thesaurus, shortly before you were born."

"Quaaaaooooo," snorted Brenda, in a threatening manner.

"Keep your humped monstrosity away," Bone scowled, waving his hand at Brenda. "And the pile of feathers, too. I should not like to catch some horrible disease of the animal or bird kingdom. Heaven forbid!"

"RAAAAAAARK!"

"Enough, Bone." Jim walked towards his nemesis. "You've had a huge shock, and you—"

Savagely, Bone sprang at Jim. "Shock? Me, a shock? I'll show *you* a shock!"

He reached into the pocket of his plus fours, and whipped out his Bulgarian Telescopic Scimitar. With a flick of his thumb, the blade shout out, and even more quickly, Bone leapt at Jim, spinning him around and pinioning his arm forcefully against his back.

"Now," whispered Bone, pressing the sharp blade of the Bulgarian Telescopic Scimitar against the tender flesh of Jim's neck, *"who's wearing nasty trousers? Arrrrr!"*

Doris raised her wings, furiously. "Let him go, you underhanded dregbucket!"

Bone pressed the blade harder against Jim's throat. Jim winced as the cold yet hot edge of the steel brought the blood to the surface of his neck.

"What did you say, you meddling macaw?" growled Bone.

"SHE SAID, LET HIM GOHHHHHH," came a voice, deep and thunder-like, from the doorway at the end of the gallery.

◈ ◇ ◈ ◇ ◈ 18 ◈ ◇ ◈ ◇ ◈

MISUNDERSTOOD

THE VOICE rolled into the gallery, filling every corner on the ground and every niche high in the vaulted ceiling.

Bone swung around, still holding Jim firmly with the scimitar to his throat.

When he saw what had spoken, the weapon dropped from his fat hand, and slowly, his fingers trembling, he released his grip on Cairo Jim.

Brenda turned to face the doorway. When she and Doris beheld what stood there, they could not utter a snort or a squawk. Great waves of incredulity washed over them both.

Jim staggered from Bone's grasp, his eyes filled with the enormousness of the shape in the doorway. He, too, was unable to make any sound.

Even Desdemona, up in the ceiling, suffered a major bout of silence, as her eyeballs nearly throbbed all the way out of her skull.

There, hulking against the arched door opening, stood an enormous man. He was as tall as one-and-a-half men, and his shoulders as wide as the shoulders of four men standing together.

Rock-hard muscles covered his body, which was naked, except for a small cloth – to Doris, it looked like

leather, light tan-coloured leather – covering his loins.

The most amazing thing about this man, however, was not his immense height or size or physique. It was his head and neck and upper shoulders.

The beam of his shoulders was covered with a thick mat of dark hair, which hung down across his upper arms and covered the top of his back and chest. This hair continued up his neck, and further up, covering most of his huge head...

The huge, horned head of a bull!

Jim's mouth was as dry as the Sahara. He gulped and swallowed, trying to get his tongue to work. "You ... you," he stammered, "are alive?"

The Minotaur, the ancient beast of legend, bowed his huge head slowly, like a planet falling through the universe. He raised it again, and looked at them with large, sorrowful eyes of the deepest green.

"And," said Jim, finding more of his voice, "you can ... speak!"

"I caaaaan," answered the creature, his voice coming like a wall of ocean wave, filling the gallery again. "I am part humaaaaaaaan."

"And," Jim continued, "you speak our language!"

"I am also part god. My father was Poseiiiiiiiidon. Language is nohhhhh barrier to the gods."

"Heavens to the Goddess Betsy," whispered Bone, inching closer to Jim so that he could hide behind him. "To think, that after all this time, it has survived down here ... we must be careful, Jim. We must get away

from here. This monster will tear us all to shreds, at any second!"

"No," said Jim, softly. "I don't get that feeling."

The Minotaur turned his head, and heaved his valley-like shoulders in Bone's direction. "I HAVE survived, all this time, oh, bearded one. I have been fated," he said in deep, rolling tones, "to live forevvvvvver. I keep watch over the maaaaaze. I keep watch over all of Eternityyyyyyyy…"

Brenda gave a quiet snort: now she knew what it was that she had seen, that shadow against the darkness, high up in the slit in the wall of the gallery of the double axes.

The Minotaur heard her snort. Slowly, mightily, he walked towards her, his footsteps resonating against the floor with a deep clunking sound.

"I saw thee, oh beast of many burdens," he spoke. "I saw how thou demonstrated braaaaavery. Forgive the axes. Forgive meeeee. I knew not that thou was trapped until I heard the axes' motion. I came with haste to set thee freeeeeee…"

"Rark!" exclaimed Doris. "So that was how we got through!"

"And thee," swelled the Minotaur's voice, as he turned his head and his great flared nostrils towards Jim. "Thou who were prepared to give his own liiiiife to save the life of the beast. I saw this, toooooo…"

"What's he bellowing about?" Bone whispered to Jim.

"Shhh. I'll tell you later."

Doris, still on Brenda's head, between her ears, plucked up her courage and spoke. "May I address you, oh great Minotaur?"

The creature turned back to her and Brenda, and bowed his head like a setting sun between two mountains.

"The stories we know about you," Doris said. "Are they true?"

"What stories," the Minotaur asked, "dost thou speak of, bird of bolllllldness?"

"That you killed all those young people every nine years, the young people sent down here by King Minos to be sacrificed to you?"

The creature raised his head, and his eyes were full of tears. "This is untrue," he said, his voice rolling like faraway thunder. The walls in the gallery pulsated with the sound. "I, the creature created for revvvvvenge, have never killed a living soul. It is true, bird of boldness, that every niiiiine years Minos the King sent seven young men and seven young women down here. It is true that Minos the King built this Labyrinth to keeeeeep me imprisoned, so that my detestable body, and my hideous face, would never be seen again by those on the earth, or in the heavens, or under the seeeeeas.

"But, as for the young people... I did not harm the young people... I left them alone, to try to find their own ways out of this prisonnnnn."

Jim thought back to the skeletons they had found earlier. Now he understood why they had looked so

intact. They had never been able to find their way out.

"And the story of Theseus," said Doris. "That was also an exaggeration?"

"I remember brave Theseus," answered the Minotaur. "He and I agreed that if he and his friends found their way out of here, he would tell everyone that he had slain me. It was hoped by meeeee that if this was believed up on your earth, then I would be left alonnnnne…"

The creature swung his head from side to side, and clenched his powerful fists.

"Daedalus," he said, "made the Labyrinth unlike any place ever known. I spent the first fifty years of my imprisonment trying to find the waaaaay out. I walked without sleep, I searched every corridor and passageway and room that had been built. But then, after all that tiiiiime, after all that time of not growing any older – another of my fates – I realiiiiised that my search was useless. I was doomed to remain down here. That was my destiny, foretold by all the gods…"

The Minotaur raised a great hand, and banged it heavily against his muscle-packed chest. "I did not *ask* to be fashioned thus. Is it my fault that I am part human, part animal? Is it my fault that I have been locked away, having done no injustice to the world, having committed no criiiiiime?"

Jim, Doris and Brenda listened, as did Desdemona, high above. Bone began rummaging in his pockets for a cigar.

"Why is it," the Minotaur asked, his voice heavier and deeper, "why is it that humanity imprisons those it considers different? Those it thinks are less important? I am part human. I feel, as thou do. I wish for love and safety and companionship, as thou do. I did not seek to come into this world, thus fashioned. Why did they lock me up, for so long, WHEN ALL I HAVE DONE IS TO LIVE?"

Cairo Jim felt great sadness that such things still happen to people and animals today.

"ALL I WISH FOR," lamented the Minotaur in a sudden burst of anguish, his voice clapping against the mirror walls as he bellowed, "is to know love – to taste its power … the power that has eluded me forevvvvvver!"

Jim, Doris and Brenda listened, their hearts awash with the Minotaur's plight. Even Desdemona had something of an inkling of what he meant.

Bone, however, was still trying to find a cigar. "Confound these pockets … must have a hole in … arrrr, here we are."

He took out a Belch of Brouhaha and put it to his fleshy lips. Then he started patting his waistcoat, trying to find his cigar-lighter. "Oh, blast it!"

The Minotaur's green eyes narrowed. "What," he asked, "troubles the bearded one?"

Jim moved away from Bone, so the Minotaur could fully see him.

"I've lost something," Bone snarled. "Something to light my cigar."

"A flame?" asked the creature.

"Arrrr."

"Then you shall have it." Raising his right arm, he opened its fist and pointed at Bone with his huge fingers.

A swift, lightning-thin bolt of extreme heat shot out from the creature's hand. The flame zapped across the gallery and struck the end of Bone's cigar so fiercely that Bone was flung backwards against the wall.

"Oooof! What on earth?"

"Scrark!" rasped Desdemona, above. "He lit yer cigar for ya!"

Cairo Jim put his pith helmet back on. "Such force," he gasped. "Such power!"

"Rark!" rarked Doris, astonished.

"Quaaaooooo!"

"It is within me," the Minotaur said. "The only gift from Poseiiiiiiiiidon ... from the realm of the gods. He gave it to me with the curse."

Bone puffed maniacally on the cigar as he realised the overwhelming strength possessed by the Minotaur. A plan skidded recklessly into the fleshy man's mind – a plan that would mean that the whole expedition would not have been wasted.

"Arrrr," he said, approaching Jim and the Minotaur. "To think that all the time, the power that I have been seeking is right here, right beneath my nose."

"What are you babbling about?" asked Jim.

"Shut up and let me speak." Bone stepped in front of

Jim, so that he was closer to the creature. "Oh, mighty Minotaur of marvels," he smarmed, "I think I may be able to quench your despair."

"What speakest thou?" asked the Minotaur, his hairy nostrils dilating to expel blasts of cold, frosty air.

"I think I know a way for you to come forth into the society of the human."

"Speak further, bearded mannnn…"

"Well, if you were to accompany me to the surface of the earth," said Bone, his lips curling into a false and flabby smile, "I can promise you that you shall have your revenge on the piteous garbage heap we call "humankind". I shall lead you forth, and together, Minotaur and mentor – me, Neptune Flannelbottom Bone – we shall crush the ignorant, the tasteless, the descendants of all who have imprisoned you!"

"Bone!" Jim whispered. "What are you talking about?"

Bone puffed a column of smoke into Jim's face, and his eyes flashed cruelly. "Seeing as how you and your little entourage will shortly be entombed down here by my brilliant self, I shall tell you what I have in mind." He lowered his voice so that only Jim could hear. "I shall emerge on the earth in the guise of a sideshow owner, Phineas T. Bunkum, and I shall announce that I have the very Minotaur of Crete in my sideshow. I shall hire the greatest theatre in the world – no, make that the hugest stadium – and I shall charge a phenomenal amount of money for people to see the monster. Then, when the stadium is full of the rich

and curious, I shall set loose the Great Minotaur, and threaten those present with a grisly and slow death if they do not kneel before me. This will only be the start of things, you just wait—"

"You've finally lost it, haven't you?" Jim said.

"Oh I *have*, have I?" Bone swept down and snatched up his scimitar. "I think *you* are the one about to lose it, Cairo Jim!"

With the speed of an angry tiger, Bone flashed the scimitar through the space between himself and Jim. The point pierced Jim's shirt, and, in the next second, just as it was going deeper—

—another huge blast of flame shot from the Minotaur's hand, hitting Bone smack-bang in the chest, and hurling him all the way to the other end of the gallery.

"AAAWWWUUUULLLLLGGGGGHHHHHHH!" he wailed, dropping the scimitar as he sprawled through the air.

"I HEAR ALL," the Minotaur bellowed, his voice clanging against the walls, stretching them almost to buckling point. "I SAW ALL. I SAW YOU AND YOUR DETESTABLE WAYYYYYYYYS…"

"Scrark!" wailed Desdemona, looking down on the scene. "I ain't hangin' around ta be barbecued meself! I'm outta here!"

She opened her wings and shot off, across the upper reaches of the gallery and down through the doorway, her candle sputtering as she flew.

Bone picked himself up and furiously patted down his singed clothing. "Arrrrr, you hideous monster!" he shouted. "How dare you—"

The Minotaur pushed his hand out further, and another flame-spout poured forth.

"NOOOOOO!" wailed Bone, as he fled in Desdemona's wake, rubbing the Prime Ministers on his bottom. "You have not heard the last of me, I promiiiissse!"

The flame sparked off Bone's rump and hit the edge of the doorway to the cavern, and petered out to nothing.

Then the Minotaur turned to Jim, Doris and Brenda. "I know," he said to them, "that there exist good people and bad people. As old as I am, as old as these rocks are, such things wilt always be the saaaaame."

"Indeed they will," said Jim, sadly.

"I must leave thy presence," the Minotaur said. "I must go. My existence stretches before me. Unlike poor Talos here" – the Minotaur swept his arms wide open, across the floor of the gallery – "I shall live onnnnn. I wish thee success in finding thy way out of here, and may the ancient things of goodness remain with thee. Farewell, sir."

"But," Jim said. "When we *do* find our way out of here … well, why don't you come with us?"

The Minotaur locked his lamp-like eyes on the archaeologist-poet. For some long moments he said

nothing. Then he shook his head. "No," he rumbled. "My heart is not meant for your world. Farewell, sir."

"Farewell," Jim said.

"Farewell, beauuuuutiful bird."

Doris lowered her beak, her heart heavy for the Minotaur.

"Farewwwwwell, noble, brave beast."

"Quaaaoooo," Brenda snorted. She above all sensed the deep loneliness of the creature as he turned and made his way out of the gallery.

"Minotaur?" called Jim, just as he was about to turn the corner and leave them.

The Minotaur turned, and raised his horned head.

"Please, may I ask you one last thing?"

"Mmmmm," came the rolling answer.

Jim took off his pith helmet. "What is it that has kept your spirit alive for so long? Is it divine intervention? Is it part of the curse?"

"No," answered the creature, after a long silence. "It is neither of those things. It is a simple thing. Small. Small, yet at the same time, bigger, more enormous, more substantial than any of the gods from my ancient world."

Doris looked down at Brenda. Even the Wonder Camel did not know what the Minotaur meant.

"Even greater, this small thing," the Minotaur said, "than *all* of the gods under the arm of Zeus Himself. Greater than Poseidon's mightiest wave..."

The creature lowered his head to his chest, and

seemed to be thinking for a brief time. Then, slowly, like the moon rising over deep, dark hills, he raised his head above his valley-like shoulders.

"This thing," he rumbled, "has never left me. This thing that has kept me aliiiive, here in the glooooom and forgotten darkness."

"What – please tell us," said Jim. "What is this thing of which you speak, yet name it not?"

Fixing his eyes again on Jim of Cairo, the maligned and misunderstood Minotaur uttered the one word that had sustained him…

And his voice rolled in like a thousand gentle rolls of thunder:

"HOPE."

The echo swelled.

Hope

    Hope

        Hope…

The creature lowered his head again. With heavy footsteps, he slipped into the deep, disappearing blackness of the Labyrinth's furthest reaches.

THE EMBERS OF DAWN

TWO DAYS LATER, the marble slab concealing the entrance to the Labyrinth was pushed and heaved across the earth.

Out of the hole sprang Doris, her yellow and blue wings shining brightly in the early-morning sunlight. "Raark! Terra firma again! Whacko!" She waddled around the ruins, lifting her beak to the rising sun and blinking at the daylight.

Next clambered Brenda, up and out of the hole. She had a quick canter across the courtyard, kicking up her hoofs with joy at being above ground again.

Finally, his pith helmet dented and his arms and legs bruised, came the archaeologist-poet. He hoisted himself up and sat at the lip of the hole, breathing in the fresh air of morning.

Doris came waddling up to him. "So," she squawked. "What now?"

"Quaaaooo?" snorted Brenda, nuzzling his back with her snout.

Jim put on his special desert sun-spectacles and stretched his arms. "I think," he said, "we've got a few bits of legend to straighten out, don't you?"

"Rark!"

"Quaaaooo!"

"There's some right to be put back into the world. A reputation needs fixing."

He stood and took off his knapsack. As he extended his arm, Doris hop-fluttered up onto it, and then walked its length to sit on his shoulder.

"Sometimes," he said, tousling the macaw's plumage and stroking Brenda's snout, "we find treasures that are different from the ones we think we're looking for. Wouldn't you agree?"

"Indubitably," said Doris, blinking.

"Just what I was thinking myself," thought Brenda the Wonder Camel.

"Time to go, then."

And, as the three made their way across the grounds of the Palace of Knossos, a low, distant rumbling, too distant for them to hear, sighed through the earth and what lay beneath it, far, far below.

THE END